You're About to Become a
Privileged Woman.

INTRODUCING
PAGES & PRIVILEGES™.

It's our way of thanking you for buying
our books at your favorite retail store.

GET ALL THIS FREE
WITH JUST ONE PROOF OF PURCHASE:

◆ **Hotel Discounts** up
to 60% at home and
abroad ◆ **Travel Service**
- Guaranteed lowest
published airfares
plus 5% cash back
on tickets ◆ **$25 Travel Voucher**

$50 VALUE

◆ **Sensuous Petite Parfumerie** collection

◆ **Insider Tips Letter**
with sneak previews
of upcoming books

*You'll get a FREE personal card, too.
It's your passport to all these benefits– and to
even more great gifts & benefits to come!*

There's no club to join. No purchase commitment. No obligation.

D1051699

Enrollment Form

☐ *Yes!* I WANT TO BE A *Privileged Woman.*

Enclosed is one *PAGES & PRIVILEGES*™ Proof of Purchase from any Harlequin or Silhouette book currently for sale in stores (Proofs of Purchase are found on the back pages of books) and the store cash register receipt. Please enroll me in *PAGES & PRIVILEGES*™. Send my Welcome Kit and FREE Gifts -- and activate my FREE benefits -- immediately.

More great gifts and benefits to come like these luxurious Truly Lace and L'Effleur gift baskets.

▶ DETACH HERE AND MAIL TODAY! ◀

NAME (please print)
_____

ADDRESS _____ APT. NO _____

CITY _____ STATE _____ ZIP/POSTAL CODE _____

PROOF OF PURCHASE
~~SAMPLE ONLY~~

Please allow 6-8 weeks for delivery. Quantities are limited. We reserve the right to substitute items. Enroll before October 31, 1995 and receive one full year of benefits.

NO CLUB!
NO COMMITMENT!
Just one purchase brings you great **Free Gifts and Benefits!**
(More details in back of this book.)

Name of store where this book was purchased_____

Date of purchase_____

Type of store:

☐ Bookstore ☐ Supermarket ☐ Drugstore

☐ Dept. or discount store (e.g. K-Mart or Walmart)

☐ Other (specify)_____

Pages & Privileges™

Which Harlequin or Silhouette series do you usually read?
_____

Complete and mail with one Proof of Purchase and store receipt to:

U.S.: *PAGES & PRIVILEGES*™, P.O. Box 1960, Danbury, CT 06813-1960

Canada: *PAGES & PRIVILEGES*™, 49-6A The Donway West, P.O. 813, North York, ON M3C 2E8

PRINTED IN U.S.A

> **"What are you doing in my room dressed like that?"** the man asked.

"Like what?" Tory demanded.

"Like a—a man."

"Thanks," Tory sputtered. Her appearance had been described in a number of ways by attractive men, but *masculine* hadn't been one of them. "It's *my* room. Remember?"

Fortunately, a key sounded in the lock. *Probably security,* Tory hoped. But it was only the housekeeper, Emma, who pushed a cart into the room, whisked away a linen cloth and revealed breakfast for two.

"I brought you and Mr. Randolph Trent a nice breakfast," Emma said.

Tory gasped. "You know him?"

"His picture's in the west hallway," Emma returned.

"But those pictures are a hundred years old," Tory exclaimed. "Randolph Trent would be—"

"Dead." Emma's eyes sparkled. "As a doornail."

Dear Reader,

This month a new "Rising Star" comes out to shine, as American Romance continues to search for the best new talent...the best new stories.

Let me introduce you to Charlotte Douglas. When we asked her about her inspiration for *It's About Time*, she had this to say, "From childhood, I have attended social functions at a grand Victorian hotel that overlooks the Gulf of Mexico from a bluff near my home. Its gingerbread trim and Tiffany stained-glass windows conjure up images of what life was like when the hotel was new. Writing *It's About Time* gave me the opportunity to put those fantasies into words. I still live near the Gulf with my high school sweetheart, whom I married over three decades ago, and enjoy weaving stories of the Florida I love."

Turn the page and catch a "Rising Star"!

Sincerely,

Debra Matteucci
Senior Editor & Editorial Coordinator
Harlequin Books
300 East 42nd Street, 6th Floor
New York, New York 10017

Charlotte Douglas

Douglas

IT'S ABOUT TIME

Harlequin Books

TORONTO • NEW YORK • LONDON
AMSTERDAM • PARIS • SYDNEY • HAMBURG
STOCKHOLM • ATHENS • TOKYO • MILAN
MADRID • WARSAW • BUDAPEST • AUCKLAND

ISBN 0-373-16591-9

IT'S ABOUT TIME

Chapter One

"How 'bout a nice cuppa tea, m'dear? You look all done in."

Tory Caswell glanced up in surprise. The last of the wedding guests had left an hour ago and she'd believed herself alone in the deserted ballroom, too tired to move, too depressed to face her lonely hotel room.

Hovering at her elbow, the small, elderly woman in a maid's uniform seemed to have appeared from nowhere. "Won't take but a minute to fix it."

Tory strained to see the woman's face in the muted darkness of the cavernous hall, but discerned only the silhouette of her slight figure, backlighted by the faint glow from tiny white lights strung along the ballroom's cornices and carved columns.

"No, thanks," Tory said. "Everything's taken care of here. I'll be leaving soon."

The maid glanced around the room which was festooned with greenery, cream-colored streamers, blush roses and pink-tinged lilies.

Jill's wedding colors—the colors of St. Valentine's Day.

As the older woman shifted position, the soft light illuminated rosy cheeks, brilliant lavender eyes and a luminous coronet of white hair above the serviceable gray and white of her uniform. "Must have been a lovely wedding," she mused.

"Yes." A sigh heavy with sadness escaped before Tory could suppress it. "My sister's."

"You look like a bride yourself, m'dear. Rose satin and creamy lace. What do you call that style?" The woman reached out a tentative hand and touched Tory's mutton sleeve.

"Victorian. My sister's crazy for it. That's why she chose this old hotel for her wedding." A tear slipped from Tory's eye and slid down her cheek.

"Here, now." The little woman withdrew a linen handkerchief from her apron pocket and pressed it into Tory's hand. "Weddings are supposed to be happy events."

"This one was—" Tory sniffed "—but my sister and her husband are going to live in his home in Australia. They left right after the reception. I'm really going to miss her."

"Of course, you will, but life has a way of bringing surprises to fill those empty spaces." The maid's kind, lilting voice with its British accent and warm tones eased Tory's pain. "Let me bring you that cup of tea. I'll have one myself, and you can tell me all about the wedding."

"Please, don't trouble—"

"No trouble at all, Miss Caswell. By the way, me name's Emma, and I'll be back with the tea before you can blink."

The tiny woman skittered away on silent, sensible shoes and disappeared through the swinging door that led to the kitchen.

How did Emma know her name? A strange shiver of apprehension tingled along Tory's spine, until she reminded herself that the maid must have heard her being introduced along with the rest of the wedding party at the start of the elaborate reception.

The planning and preparation of the grand event were all behind her now. Two weeks of glorious, hard-earned vacation in the Florida sun stretched before her. She hadn't taken time off in years, but the advertising firm she'd worked so hard to build could rock along without her while she recharged her batteries and readied herself for the corporate fray once again. The morning's weather report had forecast sleet and ice for Atlanta, but the brief early February cold spell holding Florida in its chilly grip would be history by tomorrow afternoon, the cheerful TV weatherman had promised.

She'd spend Sunday basking on the beach, reading the bestseller she'd packed with her swimsuit and bridesmaid's gown. With luck, she'd meet an attractive, unattached male ready for a brief romance. Nothing permanent. She couldn't divert the time from her work. Just a few days of sand, sea and sunshine in the arms of a handsome distraction.

She stood, shook out her long skirt and crossed the wide floor of gleaming oak. Dimly lighted panels of Tiffany stained glass arched high over linen-draped tables, which were topped with miniature topiaries of roses and baby's breath and ringed the dance floor in perfect formation.

The dusty pink of the decorations had been her mother's favorite color. Tory's throat clenched with grief. Her parents hadn't lived to see Jill married.

She leaned stiff and unyielding against the tall windows and gazed out over landscaped grounds that dipped to the Gulf of Mexico. A full moon hung above the calm water, trailing a silver swath from horizon to the shore.

Ever since the family had vacationed there when she and Jill were children, her sister had dreamed of a romantic Florida wedding in the century-old Bellevue Hotel with its gabled roofs and broad verandas with gingerbread trim.

"Your dreams came true, Jillie." She spoke aloud, and her words echoed in the immense room. "Maybe mine would, too, if I knew what they were."

Suddenly an icy current of air invaded the room, and the hair rose on the back of Tory's neck. Feeling uneasy, she returned to her table for her handbag, ready to forgo tea with the sprightly Emma and call it a night.

She stopped short at the sight of a woman silhouetted against the double doors at the far end of the room.

"May I help you?" Tory called, thinking one of the wedding guests had returned to retrieve a forgotten purse or wrap.

Silently, the woman advanced. She hadn't been a guest. Tory had never seen her before. The strikingly beautiful creature with chalk white skin and luxurious black hair cascading in ringlets wore a costume similar to Tory's bridesmaid's dress. Its turquoise silk shimmered with an iridescent brilliance that drew all other illumination from the room, and an eerie light shone from her pale blue eyes as she glided across the polished dance floor, leaving a wake of darkness in her path.

As she moved nearer, the air turned frigid, and Tory shuddered from the cold—and the look of undisguised misery in the young woman's eyes. Tory glanced nervously toward the kitchen door, but none of the hotel staff was in sight.

The young woman lifted a pale, slender hand and stabbed a thin finger at Tory. "Have you seen him?"

"Seen who?" Tory asked. The newcomer had a high sense of melodrama, but she made little sense. Had the stranger had too much to drink?

The woman moaned, a thin, pitiful sound. "The man I'm going to marry."

"No, and after tonight," Tory said with a weary sigh, "I want nothing to do with weddings for a long time."

The temperature in the room seemed to plummet and Tory's teeth began to chatter. The hotel must have shut down the heat in the ballroom as soon as the last guest departed.

"Please help me," the woman pleaded. "I must find him."

"Everyone left over an hour ago. If he was here, he's long gone." Tory started toward the door, but the woman blocked her way.

"He can't be gone. I need him." Sobs shook the young woman's delicate frame and tears tracked her pale cheeks.

Tory opened her mouth to call for help, planning to place the distraught young woman in the care of the hotel staff, but before she could utter a sound, the blue-clad figure collapsed, weeping, onto the ballroom floor... and evaporated into the frigid air.

Tory stared at the empty dance floor. People didn't just disappear into thin air. There had to be a reasonable explanation for the phenomenon she'd witnessed. She sank onto the nearest chair, wondering if she'd drunk more champagne than she'd realized. An alcoholic hallucination, that's what she'd seen. Or maybe she was just suffering from fatigue. Her staff had warned her she'd been working too hard.

A sharp noise rang out, and she started at the sound of Emma banging through the door from the kitchen with a large tea tray.

Emma settled the tray on the table with a thump and eyed Tory sharply. "Something's wrong."

"No." Tory reached for her beaded handbag with trembling hands and rose from her chair. "I'm just tired. I'm going to bed."

"You look as if you've seen a ghost."

"I don't believe in such things!" Tory winced at the sharpness of her reply.

"So you *have* seen her. I knew she'd make an appearance tonight." Emma gripped Tory's elbow and guided her to her seat, patting her arm with a soft, plump hand. "Drink your tea—it's my own special brew—and tell me all about it."

Tory inhaled deeply to calm her jangled nerves. Warm air, scented with roses and lilies, wafted through the room, a soothing contrast to the surreal cold and darkness that had filled the space only minutes before.

Then Emma's meaning struck her. "You knew she'd be here? How?"

"The ghost—"

"I don't believe in ghosts," Tory repeated, more to herself than Emma. She drank deeply of the fragrant tea, noting its exotic flavor as her tensions slid away.

"Of course you don't." Emma's amethyst eyes twinkled in the soft light. "But anyone who meets our Angelina soon becomes a believer."

"Angelina?"

"For almost a century, every time there's a wedding at the Bellevue, Angelina makes an appearance." Emma, her forehead creased in thought, dumped sugar in her tea. "But usually it's the bride she confronts."

"Thank God that—that—*apparition* didn't spoil Jillie's day! Who—what is she?"

"Almost one hundred years ago, shortly after the Bellevue first opened, Angelina Fairchild spent the season here. She fell in love with another guest at the hotel, but they quarreled."

Tory took another sip of tea and eyed the little woman over the rim of her cup. "How do you know all this?"

"It's part of the local lore." Emma smoothed her spotless apron across her lap. "You can see Angelina for yourself in the historical exhibit in the west hall. She's in several pictures, one astride a bicycle in front of the west portico."

"Most lovers quarrel at some time or another, but they don't haunt brides for a century after they die." Tory struggled to stay awake. The demands and excitement of her long day had caught up with her.

Leaning across the table like a conspirator, Emma dropped her voice to a whisper. "This was no ordinary quarrel. Angelina stormed out of the hotel afterward, down to the waterfront, and set off toward the island alone in a sloop."

Tory stifled a yawn with the back of her hand. "Nothing unusual in that. Maybe she wanted to put some distance between her and her lover, clear her head."

"The story doesn't end there. The sloop capsized in a freak wind and Angelina drowned." Emma poured more tea into Tory's cup. "The lovers never had a chance to reconcile. Ever since that tragic night Angelina has haunted weddings at the hotel, searching for her lost love, trying, I suppose, to set things right again.''

Recalling the desperate gleam in Angelina's pale eyes, Tory shivered in the warm room, then gulped the rest of her tea. ''You tell a hell of a bedtime story, Emma. I hope it doesn't keep me awake.''

Emma patted her hand and smiled sweetly. ''Nonsense, m'dear. You'll sleep like a baby. I guarantee it.''

Tory stumbled wearily across the ballroom. At the doors that led into the hall, she turned to survey one last time the scene of her sister's wedding, happy all had gone well, glad it was over. Emma and her tea tray were nowhere in sight. A chill raced down her spine at the little maid's instant disappearance, and she fled into the dark, deserted hallway.

''Where is he? Where is he?'' Whispers surrounded her in the gloom, chanting in her ear. Her skin prickled at the menace in the sound.

She flattened her back against the wall of the hallway and peered up and down the corridor for the origin of the voices. When she stood still, the murmurs ceased. She pushed away from the wainscot, scurrying down the long, dim corridor to her room as quickly as her lengthy skirts allowed.

The whispers followed. *''Where is he? Where is he?''*

She fumbled with her room key, locked her door behind her and leaned against it. Again, the voices ceased. When she walked toward her bed, they began again as her voluminous satin skirts swished around her ankles, making a whispering sound, and she laughed at her sudden attack of nerves. The fleet-footed Emma had simply disappeared into the kitchen, and the plaintive voices were no more than the rustling of her own skirts.

As for Angelina, since she turned up only at weddings, Tory had seen the last of her. Her emotional turmoil stemmed from the strain of Jill's wedding and subsequent departure—not anything supernatural.

Sleep, that was what she needed. She reached to unzip her gown but her arms refused to respond to her commands. Her head lolled on her shoulders as if it weighed a ton. Abruptly the room tipped and reeled around her until, still wearing her wedding clothes, she sprawled across the wide poster bed and drifted into oblivion.

She dreamed of Jill's wedding. The ceremony and reception unfolded before her like a video recording of the day's events, until the bridal party stepped onto the hotel veranda to where the limousine waited to take Jill and Rod to the airport. Then reality faded. Instead of late evening darkness, the Florida sun shone high in the heavens.

As she stood alone on the hotel drive, waving until her sister disappeared from view, she glanced toward the barrier islands, strips of green along the western horizon, now strangely empty of hotels and condominiums.

The sound of hoofbeats drew her attention down the palm-lined avenue that led from the heavy entrance gates to the hotel. A lone rider approached at a canter, moving in slow motion through the shimmering air.

Sunlight glinted on his light brown hair, shaggy and long against the opening of his collarless shirt. The tanned muscles of his arms, exposed by sleeves rolled to his biceps, tensed as he handled the reins. Even from a distance, eyes like burnished pewter burned into hers with a searching stare, anchoring her feet beneath her.

Held fast by his gaze, she watched him advance, gauging the width of his broad shoulders and the strength of his jodhpur-clad thighs gripping the saddle. The sun's heat flared in the pit of her stomach as the rider urged the chestnut stallion into a gallop and bore down toward her. Her feet ignored her command to turn and flee. She opened her mouth to scream but could make no sound.

The rider drew closer. Iridescent beads of sweat rolled from his wide brow down the sharp angle of his jaw, the stallion's hot breath seared her face, and still the horseman advanced.

She heard her own voice assuring her she was only dreaming, and her feet remained fixed against her struggle to flee as the huge beast with its handsome rider crashed into her, knocking her to the ground, where blackness encompassed her.... The trill of a mockingbird in a cypress tree outside her window awakened her. Midmorning light flooded the room. She struggled to rise, but a weight across her body held her firm. Turning her head, she confronted a tanned face against the stark whiteness of her pillow. The man from her dream slept beside her.

Chapter Two

Rand Trent moaned as sledgehammers pounded his brain. He didn't remember drinking much the night before, just wine with dinner and brandy afterward as he'd discussed business with Jason Phiswick in the hotel dining room. He vaguely recalled a hotel servant hovering at his elbow, refilling his glass, and a precarious trip on wobbly legs to his room.

The glare of Florida sunlight pierced his closed eyelids, increasing the tempo and volume of his head's incessant hammering. As he turned onto his stomach, he realized he still wore the clothes he'd donned for dinner the previous evening, shoes and all.

"Damn and blast." He groaned and buried his face in his pillow to shut out the light as he clasped a soft bundle of satin blanket closer to his side.

A startled gasp in his left ear brought him out of the feathered depths with a jerk that sent pain flashing through his temples. On the pillow beside him, eyes the color of the Gulf of Mexico at noon stared at him from a delicate face filled with fright.

He watched in fascination as the blue green eyes screwed shut, remaining closed for an instant while the woman's breathing eased. Then one thickly-lashed eyelid opened hesitantly, and she scrutinized him with what appeared to be disbelief. Then both eyes and her soft, full lips opened wide in prelude to a shriek.

Bloody hell. The woman was about to cause a scene. With a fluent motion and his head screaming in protest, he levered himself over the startled female to the edge of the bed and crushed his lips to her mouth to stifle her cry.

For a moment her lips yielded to the pressure of his, and her body, scented with magnolias, relaxed beneath him as he savored the taste of her. He was just beginning to enjoy himself when her clenched fists pounded on his shoulders, thrusting him away.

The force of her blows intensified the pounding in his head and soured his disposition. He drew back far enough to catch the outrage in her expression. She scrubbed her lips with the back of one hand, then opened her mouth again, as if to yell.

"Oh, no, you don't." With a lightning move, he covered her jaw with his hand, intending to oust the beautiful intruder from his room, draw the draperies against the stabbing light and bury his throbbing temples beneath his pillow once more.

"Who are you and what are you doing in my bed?" he growled at her.

Flailing her arms and legs, she struggled against his hand across her mouth. He jerked back in pain and surprise as her teeth sank into his flesh.

"Good God, woman, you should be muzzled!"

"And you should keep your hands to yourself," she snapped.

"What do you expect when you crawl into a stranger's bed?" The previous evening must have included events of which he had no memory. Struggling to remember, he dug into the pocket of his suit and fished out several crumpled bills. "This should cover whatever I owe you. Now please leave quietly so a man can get some sleep."

When he thrust the money toward her, her pupils dilated with flashing anger. She ignored the money and tugged furiously at her skirts, trapped beneath his weight on the bed's edge.

"Just get off my dress," she muttered through clenched teeth, "and I'm outta here."

Before he could brace himself, the woman shoved him, twisting away and wrenching her skirts from beneath him. He toppled off the bed's edge, rolled across the carpet and landed with a thud against the door to the hallway.

She sidled toward him, then halted when she saw he blocked the door. Scurrying to the desk on the opposite side of the room, she grabbed up a telephone he hadn't remembered being there the night before and poked the buttons atop it with long, elegant fingers.

"There's an intruder in my room. Send security!"

The edge of panic clashed with the lyrical sweetness of her voice, and he noted for the first time the rose satin evening gown that molded her trim figure. Scrambling in his memory for details of the previous evening, he could find nothing to connect him with this woman—and he would have remembered her. The honeyed tones of her thick hair, the curve of her delicate cheek and the slim yet enticing body were just to his liking.

"Who are you?" They both spoke at once.

He propped himself into a sitting position and held up his hands to assure her he meant no harm. His forehead throbbed with the worst hangover of his life, and his vision clouded as he studied her, pressed against the desk, eyeing him warily and hefting the telephone receiver as if wanting to strike him with it.

"Ladies first." He nodded toward her and struggled to keep his expression neutral. If the interest he felt showed on his face, she'd feel threatened, indeed.

"I'm Victoria Caswell and this is *my* room. How did you get in and what do you want?" Anger and indignation drove the sweetness from her voice.

He attempted to stand, but his knees refused to cooperate. Blasted hangover. Leaning against the door, he patted the pockets of his suit. "I had my key last night but I can't find it now. I must have left it in the door."

"You couldn't have a key. This is my room. Here—" She groped behind her on the desk and held up a key attached to a numbered medallion. "See? Room 131, *my* room. Now get out, or you can wait for security to arrest you. They'll be here any minute.''

Confusion joined the pounding in his head. ''But 131 is my room number—and I swear, Miss Caswell, you were not in my bed when I fell asleep last night. I'd have remembered.''

He'd sworn off women, but he wasn't dead yet. And a man would have to be stone-cold dead not to appreciate Victoria Caswell. At his words, a flush of pink only slightly lighter than her gown spread across her high cheekbones. Anger or modesty? He couldn't tell.

The woman edged to the nearby bureau, jerked open a drawer and reached inside, never taking her eyes off him. ''These should convince you this room is mine, unless you have kinky taste in underwear.''

Tory thrust the handful of blush pink lingerie toward the intruder. Where the hell were the security guards? The stranger's gaze locked speculatively on the silk teddy dangling from her fingers. Stupid move. If the man was a sex maniac, she'd just waved a red flag before a charging bull. She shoved the suggestive garment into the drawer and bumped it closed with her hip, keeping him in clear view. The instant he moved from the door, she'd make a run for it.

''Looks a bit small for me.'' His generous mouth split into a broad grin. ''And pink's not my color.''

Her breath caught at the attractiveness of his smile, and she fought the impulse to relax her guard. ''And this is not your room.''

She remembered his gray eyes from her dream, but a look of dazed confusion replaced their former piercing stare.

"Then why am I here?" He spoke softly, as if to himself, and she strained to hear him mumble, "Did you invite me in?"

She drew herself up stiffly. "I'm not in the habit of inviting drunken strangers into my bedroom, not even handsome ones."

She clasped her hand over her mouth. Was she crazy? Why had she blurted out that, even in his disheveled state, she liked the look of him?

He didn't appear to notice her compliment but slumped against the door. "My head is swimming. Could I trouble you for a glass of water?"

She would have opened the door and escaped into the hallway, but he sat between her and freedom. She noted the ashen hue of his complexion. The man appeared genuinely ill. It couldn't hurt to humor him. Anything to stall him until security arrived.

She backed into the bathroom, taking her eyes off him only long enough to fill a glass, but he remained slouched against the door as if he'd fall over if he tried to sit up straight. When she handed him the glass, his tanned fingers closed around hers, sending a strange tingle of warmth up her arm. Alarmed, she jerked away.

"Thank you." He raised the glass to his mouth with a trembling hand, then lowered the glass slowly to the floor by the door.

She breathed deeply to calm her own trembling. "Now will you please leave?"

"Not until you promise to have dinner with me this evening to make up for my—my mistake."

Her head filled with images of his handsome face across the table on the hotel terrace before her common sense kicked in once more. "You don't owe me anything, except my privacy."

He drew his hand to his mouth, sucking where her teeth had drawn blood. "You're right. I'd better go before I bleed to death."

Ignoring her twinge of sympathy, she punched the number for the front desk once more, but the line rang busy in her ear.

"There's obviously been some kind of error," he said. "Maybe we were booked into the same room by mistake." He climbed unsteadily to his feet and pushed away from the door, moving toward her.

"Stay back. I'm warning you." In a panic, she grabbed the nearest object, a leather-bound phone directory.

The man either hadn't heard or paid no attention to her words. He stumbled relentlessly toward her. When he came within arm's length, she raised the phone book and brought it down across his broad brow.

He shook his head like a dazed animal, turned toward the door and traveled only as far as the middle of the room before his knees buckled beneath him. He pitched facedown on the plush carpet and lay still.

Tory froze. She hadn't hit him that hard, and the padded leather had softened the blow. His collapse could be a ploy to draw her within his reach. The busy signal continued to ring at the front desk, and she had dialed an outside line to call emergency services when someone rapped on her door.

Relief flooded her. Security had arrived, and she could leave the handsome stranger to them.

"Come in," she called.

The door opened several inches and Emma's cheery face peeked through. "The front desk sent me, m'dear. Security's tied up with a brawl in the spa and a theft on the third floor."

Tory bit back a bitter reply. What good would a hundred-pound old lady be against her intruder? She nodded toward the unconscious form, spread-eagled on the floor. "He broke into my room during the night. I found him in my bed when I woke up this morning."

Emma scurried to the man's side. "Oh, dear, you haven't hurt him, have you?"

"He broke into my room. God knows what he intended." The maid had to be simpleminded. "I want him out of here—fast."

"I'll send security as soon as they're free and see if I can locate a doctor."

"Wait—"

The door closed behind Emma and Tory was alone with the stranger once more. She sidled past his prostrate form toward the door, intending to vacate the room until security had removed the intruder. As she backed toward the doorway, reaching behind her for the doorknob, the man moaned, a heart-wrenching sound that stopped her in her tracks.

He was obviously ill. What if her blow to his head had scrambled his senses? What if he suffered from a life-threatening illness? What if she abandoned him and he died? Besides, security would be along any minute, and in his condition what harm could he do her?

The stranger lay prone with his face turned toward her and one arm flung above his head. She knelt beside him and raked her fingers through his thick, fine hair, feeling for lumps or other signs of injury. Long lashes curled darkly against a cheek that seemed pale beneath his tan. She cupped his square jaw in her palm, then lay the inside of her wrist against his broad forehead. Cool and dry with no signs of fever.

Then she noticed his clothes—the strange cut of his gray suit, the width of his shirt collar, the odd knot in his tie and his gleaming black boots. Probably European. The majority of the hotel's guests were tourists from outside the United States. She attempted to roll him over to search his coat pockets for identification, but she couldn't budge his dead weight.

When her hand brushed a damp spot beside him, she drew back in disgust. Where his right hand touched the carpet, blood dripped from the neat half-moon of her teethmarks.

She scurried to the pristine white-tiled bathroom, squeezed cold water from two fresh facecloths, then returned to the immobile form on her bedroom floor.

Tying one cloth around his bleeding hand, she wiped his face with the other in an attempt to rouse him.

While the stranger lay unmoving, as still as death, Tory dialed the front desk again. The line rang continually, but no one answered.

"Come on, come on!" she muttered through clenched teeth.

"What is *that?*"

She jumped at his question. The stranger had regained consciousness and raised himself up onto one elbow. He was staring at the television set a few feet away.

Her heart hammered against the ecru lace of her Victorian bodice. His disorientation was even worse than she'd feared. What was keeping security? "The television? What did you think it was?"

"Didn't know. What's a television?" he groaned, as he struggled to pull himself upright and got only as far as his knees.

When he threatened to pitch forward on his face once more, she bent down, pulled his arm around her shoulders and dragged him to his feet. Staggering under his weight, she maneuvered him to her bed, where he slumped against the pillows.

His eyes, gray as a winter day, held her as his good hand grasped her wrist. "Thank you. I'm so tired...."

His eyes closed and he released his grip. She leaned forward, listened for the even sound of his breathing, then pulled a blanket from the foot of the bed across the broad expanse of his chest. With the strong contours of his face relaxed in sleep, the man appeared far less threatening than when she'd first discovered him in her bed.

Thick, fine hair of sun-burnished mahogany fell over his high forehead to his eyebrows, giving him the appealing appearance of a sleeping child, but there was nothing childlike about the hard muscles of his chest and thighs that even a thick blanket couldn't hide. Through slightly parted lips, strong white teeth gleamed and fine lines etched the corners of his mouth. A shadow of stubble darkened his firm, unyielding jaw. A man to be reckoned with.

She tore away from her study of the enigma before her. No use fantasizing over the handsome hunk fate had thrown her way. Even if his brains weren't scrambled, she had no use for him—for any man.

When her mother had died—of grief, Tory believed—shortly after her father's fatal heart attack just a year before, Tory had vowed never to become so dependent on a man's love that she couldn't live without him. Her mother had given up on life, but Tory would never let love destroy her, even if it meant remaining single the rest of her days. She had her work. What more could she want?

She gathered fresh clothes and carried them into the spacious bathroom where she locked the door behind her. As she removed her bridesmaid's gown and hung it on the back of the door, sorrow pierced her. Her sister was now halfway around the world. Jill had Rod, and his large, boisterous family would be waiting for them at the airport in Sydney. But no one would be spending the fourteen-day vacation with Tory, and no one waited in the big, two-story house in Atlanta for her return.

She glared at herself in the mirror above the sink, abhorring her self-pity. She'd done fine on her own this far, building a successful business, and she wasn't even thirty yet. She'd manage. She tried not to think of dinners with no one across the table, breakfasts with only the Atlanta *Constitution* for company and future business triumphs celebrated alone.

Alone. She wasn't alone now. She had a stranger in her room—in her bed. She eyed the shower longingly but resorted to a quick sponge bath before slipping into burgundy slacks and a shell pink blouse and tying her hair back with a plum-colored scarf. When she eased open the bathroom door, the man still lay as she'd left him, sleeping soundly in the big double bed.

But where was security? And the doctor Emma had said she'd summon? For a five-star resort, the hotel's staff had lousy response time. She punched the numbers for the front desk, only to hear the irritating buzz of the busy signal once again.

Slamming the receiver into its cradle with disgust, she looked up to find the stranger's startling gray eyes fixed on her.

"What are you doing in my room—and dressed like that?" His voice wobbled with weakness.

"Like what?"

"Like a—a man." He pulled himself into a sitting position and rubbed his temples gingerly.

"Thanks a lot," she sputtered with annoyance. "Remind me not to waste my charms on you." Her appearance had been described in various ways by a number of attentive men, but masculine hadn't been one of them. "Don't you remember? We've already established that this is *my* room."

He shook his head as if trying to clear his confusion. "I feel as if my head's been trampled by wild horses. I'm sorry—"

He paused at the sound of a key in the lock. The door to the hallway pushed open and a cart draped in a white linen cloth appeared, propelled into the room by a smiling Emma.

"What's going on here?" Tory demanded. "Where's security?"

"No need for them, m'dear. Everything's under control." Emma whipped the cloth from the cart, revealing enough breakfast for two.

"There's a stranger in my bed, no one answers at the front desk and you bring a breakfast I didn't order. That's not control, it's chaos." Tory reached for the door handle, ready to order Emma and her hearty breakfast out.

Emma thrust a glass of orange juice into Tory's outstretched hand. "I'm sure you'll feel differently once you've had your breakfast. And from the looks of him, Mr. Trent could stand a hot meal."

Tory turned from the little maid to the man who sat propped against the pillows. The color was returning to his face as he observed the two women with interest.

Then the import of the maid's words hit her. "Mr. Trent? You know him?"

"Now that I've seen his face clearly, I'd know him anywhere. Randolph Trent. I've seen his picture a thousand times in the exhibit in the west hallway." Emma bustled from the cart to the table, carrying the covered breakfast plates. "You can go check for yourself if you don't believe me."

"But those pictures were taken a hundred years ago," Tory said. "Randolph Trent is—"

"Dead—" Emma's amethyst eyes sparkled "—as a doornail."

Chapter Three

"You're out of your mind." Rand, feeling his strength surge back, swung his legs off the bed and approached the maid. "I am Randolph Trent, and although I'm a bit hung over, I'm as alive as you are."

Even as he spoke, doubts crept into his mind. Something very strange was happening to him, from the beautiful woman he'd found in his bed to the odd telephone with buttons and the curious piece of furniture she'd called a television, all in a room that had been exclusively his when he sprawled into bed the night before.

The elderly maid whipped the covers off the plates. "Of course you're alive. That's why you're hungry. But if you're not dead, there must be another explanation for your being here."

"Yes, what *are* you doing here?" the attractive young woman asked.

"*Bon appetit.*" The maid backed hurriedly out the door and closed it behind her.

"Well?" Jade eyes flashed at him, demanding an answer.

The delectable aroma of scrambled eggs and sausage assaulted his nostrils, and his stomach grumbled. He eyed the steaming breakfast longingly. How had the maid known how starved he was?

"Miss Caswell—that's right, isn't it? I feel as if I haven't eaten for days, and I don't wish to pass out on you again. Do you mind if we discuss this over breakfast in a civilized manner?"

She opened her mouth as if to protest, then seemed to think better of it and sat at the table across from him in the bay window that overlooked the rose garden. She poured coffee, while her lips clamped in a severe line, as if to staunch the flow of questions she would ask him.

He took a deep draft of coffee, hoping the stimulant would clear the cobwebs from his brains and enable him to make sense of the bizarre situation in which he found himself. His well-ordered life didn't allow for such interruptions. The sooner he could resolve the confusion over his room and return to business, the better. Distractions cost money, even so pleasing a distraction as the one across the table from him.

Tory watched him with a wary eye, still unconvinced Randolph Trent wasn't a ghost like Angelina, as he dug into the platter of sausage and eggs with all the gusto good manners allowed. Sunlight gleamed behind him through the bay window, outlining his solid silhouette. The pale Angelina had possessed a luminescent, ethereal quality. The man before her radiated robust health and the high color of dynamic flesh and blood. His eyes, unlike Angelina's pale, unhappy ones, shone with warmth and good humor.

He stared at her with a quizzical expression as he finished his second piece of toast and wiped his lips with a linen napkin. "You're not eating, Miss Caswell."

In her study of the puzzling Randolph Trent, she'd forgotten her breakfast, but the excitement churning in her stomach destroyed her appetite. "Eating can wait until you've answered a few questions. Who are you and what are you doing here?"

"I'm Randolph Trent, and I'm here at the Bellevue for a working holiday." He pushed away his plate, folded his arms on the table and leaned toward her. "I might ask the same questions. Who are you, Miss Caswell, and what are you doing here?"

Blood pounded in her temples. There had to be a rational explanation. Maybe he was Trent's great-grandson, the spitting image of his ancestor. "When did you arrive at the hotel?"

"What's today?"

"Monday."

"I arrived three weeks ago," he said, "and checked into Room 131."

Liar. She had checked into Room 131 four days ago. Then an impossible idea struck her. "What year?"

"That's a ridiculous question. The same as now, 1897, of course." He pushed back from the table and started to rise.

She felt the blood draining from her face. "But 1897 was almost a hundred years ago."

He dropped into his chair like a rock, and his face paled beneath his tan. "If you're trying to be amusing, Miss Caswell, you haven't succeeded."

"I'm not laughing, either." She reached for the remote control and flipped on the television to the weather channel. The thirty-six-hour forecast scrolled across the blue screen. "See, there in the upper right-hand corner? That's today's date."

Looking stunned, like a man who'd just suffered a devastating loss, Randolph Trent stared at the television set. "I don't believe it."

"Why would I lie?"

"No, it's not you. It's that box...." He stared at the television like a man entranced, catching his breath as the forecast gave way to a commercial filled with gurgling babies.

He rose to his feet, ran his hand over the screen, then jerked it away abruptly at the jolt of static electricity he received. Peering down the appliance's backside, he examined the cable wires connected to the wall.

"How do you do that?"

Feeling like a fairy godmother, she waved the remote control, flipping from channel to channel.

He tore his attention from the set and returned to his chair. "This must be some kind of trick. How did I get here, and what happened to the last hundred years?"

She dropped the control and settled in her chair, remembering Angelina. "Maybe you died last night."

"Oh, no." He held up his right hand, wrapped in the damp facecloth now pink with blood. "Ghosts don't bleed."

"Until last night, I didn't believe in ghosts." She looked away, distressed by the injury she'd inflicted on him. He didn't appear to intend any harm but seemed as confused as she was.

Rand folded his arms on the table and leaned toward her. "What exactly happened last night?"

"The ghost of Angelina Fairchild confronted me in the ballroom." She sipped cold coffee, avoiding the intense stare of his gray velvet eyes.

"Maybe she wasn't a ghost."

"She's a ghost, all right. Emma says—"

"Emma?" he asked.

"The maid who brought breakfast. She told me Angelina's been scaring brides here at the hotel for the last hundred years."

His eyebrows arched above eyes that widened with alarm, and he rose to his feet. "If you're a bride, then my presence places you in a compromising situation. Now that my head has ceased pounding and my lightheadedness has passed, I'll leave at once."

"No. Please, stay." Dismay at the thought of his leaving surprised her. Earlier, all she'd wanted was to be rid of the man. "I'm not the bride. My sister was married yesterday."

"I don't understand. I saw Angelina Fairchild at dinner last night—a charming young woman." He sat down and absentmindedly helped himself to another piece of toast.

Angelina's pleas rang in her mind. The man across the table knew her. Was he the man Angelina sought? Had the girl known Randolph would appear? That might explain why the ghost had accosted her and not Jill. She'd ask Emma for the name of Angelina's lost love.

Meanwhile, the possible source of Angelina's torment sat across from her. What young woman wouldn't appreciate such rugged good looks? How many other hearts had he broken? She squared her shoulders, breathed deeply and vowed not to be another trophy added to his belt.

He spooned marmalade onto his toast, started to take a bite, then paused with the bread halfway to his mouth. "Why does she haunt brides at the hotel?"

"The man Angelina loved quarreled with her. She died in an accident before they could patch things up between them. Maybe she's jealous of all brides and their happiness—or believes she'll find her own lost love in such an atmosphere."

Indignation flared his nostrils and turned his eyes to gray smoke as his teeth tore into the toast as if attacking the man who'd quarreled with Angelina. If he'd been the one who loved her, he hid it well.

"What kind of man would upset such a lovely young girl?" he asked.

"My question exactly." She considered his strong, square jaw as he chewed his food with pleasure. The very attractive flesh and blood of the man across from her played havoc with her concentration.

She leaned back in her chair to regard him more seriously. His face revealed no remorse. "But Angelina's not the problem. She only appears at weddings, so she won't be troubling me again."

"What *is* the problem—other than being out of food?" He had devoured every morsel from the serving dishes and gazed longingly at her breakfast, still untouched. "Aren't you going to eat?"

She handed him her plate and watched in astonishment as he dug into it. The man was definitely no ghost. At the rate he was eating, he would soon add a pound or two to his very real muscled bulk.

She dragged her attention to the dilemma he presented. "Problems—plural. The first being a violation of the law of physics that two bodies cannot occupy the same space."

"You mean Room 131?" He smiled across the table at her and poured fresh coffee in her cup as casually as if he always shared breakfast with a strange woman.

Her stomach fluttered as she toyed with the idea of Randolph Trent at her breakfast table every morning, then thrust aside the absurd notion. "The other problem is yours, not mine. How will you return to the Bellevue of 1897? If you can solve that one, the overcrowding in Room 131 takes care of itself."

His smile disappeared and vertical lines appeared between his thick brows as his forehead wrinkled in thought. "You might as well ask me to fly."

"Flying I can manage. The rudiments of time travel escape me."

"You can fly?" He dropped his fork and stared at her in disbelief.

"Not without a plane, of course." She stifled a giggle at the incredulous look on his face.

"Plane?"

"Huge flying machines that can carry hundreds of people through the air—but unfortunately, not through time."

He rubbed his chin thoughtfully. "Time travel—I read a book by Mr. Twain last year about such a phenomenon. A blow to the head conveyed the character to medieval England, and another blow restored him to the present. But that was fiction, of course."

"It might be worth a try." She hefted the coffeepot and eyed him speculatively.

"I applaud your enthusiasm—" his mouth split into an engaging grin "—but I remember no blow to my head last night. However, I distinctly recall entering my room, this room, and falling into bed. Besides—" he nodded toward the phone book on the dresser "—you've already attempted that solution, and it didn't work."

Her stomach flip-flopped as he smiled at her in his good-natured way. "I know nothing about time travel," she said, "but I can solve our first problem."

She carried the telephone to the table and punched in the numbers for the front desk. This time she received an immediate answer. "This is Victoria Caswell in

Room 131. I have a friend who's arrived unexpectedly and needs a room.''

Rand threw her a quizzical look when she hung up. "Well?"

"They're checking their reservations and will get back to me."

"I appreciate your efforts on my behalf, but I don't want a room. I must return where I belong. Surely a society that builds flying machines and captures moving, talking pictures in a box has some way of sending me back through time?"

She threw him a wry grin. "Not unless I can contact Dr. Who."

"Who?"

"Dr. Who is a character in a television time-travel series."

"What?"

"Never mind." Feeling like part of an Abbott and Costello routine, she gave in to laughter until she saw the disappointed look on his face.

"It's imperative that I return immediately." He rose from the table and paced the length of the suite, looking like a character from *Masterpiece Theater* in his antiquated clothing.

Her conscience nipped her. She'd been incredibly selfish, thinking only of her own inconvenience. How would she feel, thrust a hundred years into the future? Was someone searching for Randolph Trent, wondering where he'd gone? "Your family, they must be frantic."

His eyes chilled her like a winter day. "I have no one. My parents are deceased and I have no siblings."

She left the table and curled into the corner of the sofa, watching as he continued to tread the carpet from one end of the suite to the other like a powerful, caged cat. "Surely someone will miss you?"

He stopped, thought for a moment, then shook his head. "I left my valet behind in Chicago this trip. But if I'm not at the hotel to finish my negotiations by the end of the week, I stand to lose a great deal of money."

"You've been yanked forward a hundred years and all you can think of is *money?*"

The lines of his face hardened and his eyes hooded like a predator's. "Making money is what I do. I see no need to apologize for it."

"But isn't there someone you miss, who's missing you?" The warmth she'd glimpsed in him earlier had disappeared, leaving a coldness that made her shiver.

"I assure you, no one is inconvenienced by my absence, if it is brief, but my business could suffer great losses."

"I'm sorry."

But her pity was not for his bank accounts. Randolph Trent evidently had no one in his life for whom he cared deeply. He longed to return, not to his friends, but his finances. If he was the lover Angelina searched for, she should have saved herself the trouble.

Someone knocked and a moment later the hall door opened. Emma staggered in under an armload of linens, blankets and pillows.

"What are those?" Tory asked.

"You called the front desk for a room for your friend." Emma dumped her burden beside Tory on the sofa. "The hotel's full up until the end of the month, but I was able to find Mr. Trent a bed."

"Where?"

Tory hoped it would be at the opposite side of the mammoth building. There, out of sight and sound, he could rail all he wanted about losing money.

Emma's eyes twinkled like Christmas lights. "You're sitting on it, m'dear."

"What do you mean?" Tory's patience had worn thin.

"Don't worry. It's a sleeper sofa, quite comfy. Will you be needing anything else?" Emma tucked her hands beneath her apron, waiting.

"Yes, bring my bill. I'm checking out. Mr. Trent can have the suite to himself."

"No." He stopped pacing at her words. "I won't let you ruin your stay on my account. I'll find someplace else."

"Well, miss?" Emma asked.

Tory took a hard look at the man before her. His old-fashioned clothing exhibited all the signs of being slept in, and stubble darkened his strong jaw. Handsome and fit, he still resembled a homeless vagrant, which, in a way, he was. Unless his pockets were filled with gold, he hadn't enough money to live on and, even worse, no knowledge of late-twentieth-century culture. If she abandoned him now, he'd probably end up in jail or the state mental hospital. Who'd believe he was a time traveler? She wasn't sure she believed it herself.

"Never mind, Emma. I'll call the front desk when I'm ready to leave." She closed the door behind the maid, wondering if she'd done the right thing. She still didn't trust the roguishness in the man's gray eyes.

"I meant it, Miss Caswell." He loomed over her, his massive frame blocking the light. "I'll leave the room to you and find another place."

"Do you have any money?"

He emptied his pockets, rattling a few coins in his hands, handing her his checkbook, while he repocketed a large, antique gold watch.

Tory studied the checkbook. Although the paper seemed new, the checks on the Chicago bank lacked computer account numbers and printed name, address and telephone numbers.

"That may not be any good now," he said. "I don't even know if that bank still exists."

"There's one way to find out."

She dialed long-distance information and asked for the bank's number. The telephone company had no listing for such a bank, but the chatty operator volunteered that the building at that address had burned to the ground thirty years ago.

"You're out of luck." Tory returned his checkbook.

Tucking it into his pocket with the rest of his belongings, he shrugged. "Thank you for trying."

She took a deep breath. She was plunging in over her head by accepting responsibility for Randolph Trent, but she couldn't abandon him, yet. "If we're going to be roommates, call me Tory."

"Rand." He extended his hand, enveloping hers with long, powerful fingers, and a slow grin lit his face. "I'd be like a babe in the woods without someone like you to guide me. I'm grateful."

He meant every word. Without Victoria to advise him, he'd bumble like a tourist in a strange country without a guide. He'd noticed that, although he could understand her words for the most part, the cadence of her modern speech was quite different from his own, and he was certain he'd encounter new inventions that required explaining.

She seemed uncomfortable with his gratitude, unlike Selena, who had always reveled when Rand was in her debt. A faint blush singed Tory's cheeks, and her lovely eyes refused to meet his.

"Look, Rand, I need to check with the catering manager and make sure there are no loose ends from the wedding and reception yesterday." She picked up the small object that had operated the magical box, clicked on the pictures and handed it to him. "Why don't you catch up on the twentieth century while I'm gone?"

His fingers closed over her soft hand, sending a tremor of pleasure through him. Her subtle scent, an alluring mixture of magnolias and spice, teased his nostrils, and her eyes gazed at him, questioning. He grasped the control, released her hand, and the moment passed.

Emotion clogged his voice. Gratitude—that had to be it. He'd vowed after Selena he'd never let another woman touch his heart again.

He cleared his throat to speak. "An excellent suggestion."

"I'll be back soon."

The subtle swing of her hips, accentuated by her masculine trousers, riveted his attention as she crossed the room. She turned at the door with a waggle of her fingers before closing it behind her. The room seemed empty without her.

You're wasting your time, his long-dead uncle's voice echoed in his brain. *You should use every minute to full advantage. Time, after all, is money.*

The wail of a siren from the strange box she'd called a television drowned out the unwelcome reminder. He settled onto the sofa and punched buttons on the small box to change the picture. For half an hour, he watched sleek, fast horseless carriages, flying machines, foreign chefs, basketball players, a large purple creature talking with small children, and more bare arms, legs and bosoms than he'd seen in all his thirty-two years.

The longer he watched, the more aware he became of his inappropriate apparel. Unless he wanted to call attention to himself, he'd have to adopt modern clothing.

He dug into his pockets and extracted his checkbook, his watch and the fistful of change, set aside the useless bank book and counted his money. Then he picked up the telephone, punched the numbers indicated for the front desk and asked for the concierge.

TORY HURRIED BACK to the suite. Her time with the catering manager had expanded into twice what she'd expected. She'd had to sign more receipts, pay the remainder of the bill, arrange to have the wedding flowers delivered to local nursing homes and oversee the packing of the wedding cake's top layer in dry ice for its shipment to Australia, where Jill and Rod could store it in their freezer until their first anniversary—an old Southern custom and a surprise Jill wasn't expecting.

She'd also made a detour by the historic exhibit in the west wing. There, just as Emma had said, hung photographs from the hotel's early days. Prominently pictured on the steps of the west portico stood the man she'd found in her bed that morning. His high, stiff collar held his head erect as he looked toward the camera with his penetrating gaze.

But it was the woman whose hand lay possessively on his arm who caught Tory's attention. Dressed in a dark skirt, starched shirtwaist, and wearing a straw boater over her dark curls, Angelina Fairchild gazed up at Randolph Trent with laughter on her lips. On her other side stood a pleasant young man in golfing tweeds.

Tory turned toward her room. She'd ask her strange visitor again what he knew of Angelina. Two figures from the past popping into her life within a few hours of one another had to be connected somehow.

When she entered her room, the housekeeping staff had made the bed and cleaned, the breakfast dishes had been cleared, and the television was still on, as she'd left it, but the sleeping alcove and sitting area were empty. She could see through the open door that the bathroom was vacant, as well. Randolph Trent was gone.

She tried to calm her whirling thoughts. Had she dreamed his appearance? The maids must have removed the bloodstained facecloth, but on the desk beside the telephone, she found his checkbook. Rand had been in her room, all right, but now he'd disappeared.

Had the time warp that brought him winked again and carried him away? She shuddered at the thought. Would she have been whisked away with him if she'd been in the suite at the time?

Horror over her near-catastrophe turned her insides to ice, chilling her until she couldn't think straight, while outside, the blazing Florida sun drove the temperature upward.

She stripped off her clothing and pulled on her swimsuit and cover-up, anxious to escape the strange atmosphere of the hotel room and thaw her numbed brain so she could figure out what to do next. She grabbed the bestseller from her night table and fled downstairs.

Choosing a spot unshaded by palms and flowering trees near the pool, she stretched out on a lounge chair. As the sun baked the chill from her body, she thought of Randolph Trent, hoping he'd made his way safely back to 1897, trying to deny her disappointment at not saying goodbye.

Wherever he was, he was in control. From the moment she'd encountered him in her dream, she'd recognized him as a man to be reckoned with. A man like her father.

Thornton Caswell had been a take-charge person who'd run his medical practice with an iron fist. His no-nonsense approach had inspired confidence in patients about to undergo his surgery, but that same attitude had encouraged her mother to rely on him for everything, leaving her helpless after his heart attack.

Tory had stepped in to handle insurance agents, attorneys and accountants, while her mother had turned her face to the wall and died from grief.

She sighed. As attractive as Rand was, he'd been too much like her father. Just as well he'd gone back where he belonged. He had no future with her.

But the threat of unstable time in Room 131 remained. According to Emma, the hotel was booked solid, so obtaining a room change seemed unlikely.

Slowly the sun drew the tension from her muscles and relaxed her with its warmth. As she plopped over on her stomach to allow her back to tan, she considered returning to dismal, gray Atlanta. But the account for Benson, Jurgen and Ives lay waiting for her, square in the middle of her desk, and she still hadn't a single idea for a promotional campaign for the premier Southern investment firm.

What she needed was more time in the sun to re-charge her creative batteries. She'd leave the Bellevue that afternoon and head across the state to Daytona. Two weeks on the beach should banish all memories of Randolph Trent.

TINGED WITH SUNBURN and sated by a sinful cheese-burger at the poolside grill, Tory returned to her room to pack, anxious to leave Room 131 behind for good.

When she unlocked the door, Randolph Trent greeted her from the sofa, where he relaxed with his boots crossed before him on the coffee table.

"Enjoy your swim?" His eyes widened as he surveyed her from head to toe.

Conflicting emotions vied to control her. Anger won. "I'd thought you'd gone for good. Where have you been?"

A slow, easy grin, the look of a man well pleased with himself, lifted the handsome contours of his face. "Liquidating my assets. I'll need your help in cashing this."

He waved a piece of paper toward her. She snatched it angrily, provoked by the worry he'd caused her and resentful of the warm coil of pleasure spreading deep within her, triggered by his reappearance.

"My God, what have you done?" she gasped. The sight of the cashier's check for one hundred thousand dollars had driven the air from her lungs.

His grin broadened as he watched her reaction. "I needed money for clothes and other necessities."

"But how—"

"Making money is my business. Obtaining funds in an unknown environment proved challenging but not impossible."

Handling the check as if expecting it to bite her, she placed it gingerly on the coffee table and sat down across from him. "A hundred thousand dollars in a few hours? You must have used magic."

"No magic."

"You didn't rob—"

"Nothing illegal."

"Then how?"

"A resort like this one always has a most accommodating concierge."

She stared at him. "Not accommodating enough to lend you a hundred thousand dollars."

He shook his head. "I asked the concierge for the name of a bookstore and reputable coin shop, then requested he call me a cab."

He stretched lazily, lacing his fingers in the air before placing them behind his head, making his muscles ripple beneath his jacket.

She pulled her gaze from his handsome frame to the check. "Books and coins? You've lost me again."

"The cab drove me to a stationer's, where I located a book on the latest coin values. After I gathered the information I needed, the cab, which I'd asked to wait, then drove me to a large coin and jewelry shop not far from here, where I sold the contents of my pockets—including several now antique coins in both silver and gold, and my grandfather's gold pocket watch with an extremely rare seventeenth-century gold piece embedded in the fob.''

''A few coins and a watch were worth that much?''

''The total was a few hundred more, actually, but I requested the difference in cash. I needed money to pay the taxi—and tip the concierge.'' He spoke in a reasonable tone, as if acquiring a hundred thousand dollars was an ordinary occurrence.

She studied him between narrowed lids. A man to be reckoned with, all right. She'd felt sorry for him earlier, a helpless traveler from the past. Yet he hadn't been there an entire day and already had accumulated a small fortune. What could he accomplish in a week?

Her name jumped out at her from the check on the table. ''Why is the check made out to me?''

He shook his head. ''You haven't thought this through. The shop didn't have that much cash on hand, so I had to take a check.''

''That's not what I meant.''

He smiled sheepishly. ''How could I, with no identification in the present, convert such a large check to cash? You have the necessary credentials, hence the check in your name.''

She sighed. He'd thought of everything. ''Now that you have the money, what do you plan to do with it?''

He glanced at his suit and smoothed the wrinkles in his sleeve. ''As soon as I find a suitable haberdashery, I'll shop for clothes appropriate to the present.''

Like a flashbulb exploding in her brain, she pictured Rand, wearing his Edwardian suit, seated behind an antique desk, looking directly into the camera with his piercing gray eyes, spouting lines like, "Making money is what I do. I won't apologize for it."

The entire Benson, Jurgen and Ives campaign began to unfold in sequence in her imagination. If Rand was stuck in her time, she could at least give him a job—and provide her firm with the most compelling advertising model since the Marlboro Man.

A grin tugged at the corners of her mouth. "Rand, I think it's time I introduce you to the shopping mall."

Chapter Four

After changing her swimsuit for casual clothes and loafers, Tory gathered up her handbag and car keys. Rand sat in front of the television, mesmerized by a soap opera.

"Ready?" she asked.

He dragged his attention from the writhing couple on the screen. "We'll have to cash my check before I can make any purchases."

"No problem. There are banks all over. I'll stop at the nearest drive-through on our way to the mall."

He stared at her as if she was speaking Swahili. Incomprehension clouded the brilliance of his eyes. "Drive-through?"

"You'll see." She jingled her car keys at him. "We practically live in our cars. They're so important to our lives that our last war was fought over oil."

"Last? Have there been many?" Curiosity colored his words as he accompanied her down the long corridor toward the main lobby.

She counted on her fingers. "Since your time, there's been the Spanish-American, World War I, World War II, Korea, Vietnam and the Persian Gulf. That's only the ones America's been in on."

"Six wars in a century? God, we're a bloodthirsty people."

The revulsion in his voice gave her goose bumps. Humans did have a penchant for violence. So why was she going off alone with one she knew absolutely nothing about?

She cast a surreptitious glance at the man beside her, searching his chiseled profile for sinister signs. She found none, but what she observed was disturbing. The rugged beauty of the sharp planes of his jaw and cheekbones created an irresistible desire in her to trace their contours with her fingertips.

The doorman's greeting as he pulled open the massive doors with their antique beveled glass saved her from succumbing to the urge to touch the man beside her.

She halted on the veranda and drew in a deep gulp of air redolent with the tang of salt, clearing her head of fantasies. Rand Trent seemed like a nice guy. She'd help him shop and acclimate himself to the 1990s. She'd even try to sign him on as a model for her ad campaign. But she had no place in her personal life for a man with the looks of Adonis and the heart of Midas.

He stood beside her on the hotel's veranda, looking past its wicker furniture and gingerbread trim to the wall of high-rise condominiums that stood between them and the water, and shook his head sadly.

"They've ruined the landscape. Yesterday I stood in this same spot and had an unobstructed view of the islands and the gulf."

She grimaced. "We call it progress."

They descended the broad, carpeted stairs, crossed the driveway that ran beneath the portico and skirted beds of brightly colored petunias before reaching her new silver gray Toyota.

Recalling the pictures in the hotel's historical exhibit of men in stuffy clothes and women in long-skirted, high-necked dresses taking tea on the veranda, she giggled at the expression on Rand's face as a couple, carrying beach towels and dressed only in brief swimsuits, climbed into a red convertible in the parking lot.

"Progress?" He grinned at her with a devilish look.

She smiled and shook her head. "You ain't seen nothing yet."

She unlocked her car and demonstrated the seat belt to Rand, leaning across him to fasten the clasp. The nearness of him rattled her usual calm. Abruptly, she started the engine and pulled off down the broad driveway lined with towering palms and through the wrought iron entrance gates, leaving a cloud of sandy dust behind her.

In the intimacy of the car's close quarters, she struggled to keep her mind on traffic. The recirculating air of the car's cooling system filled her nostrils with the scent of leather, sunshine and sandalwood, a pervasive reminder of the man at her side.

As they drove through the city, heading for the highway that would take them north to the shopping mall she and Jill had discovered on previous visits, Rand's head snapped from side to side, taking in the tall office buildings with glass sides that reflected the Florida sky, the multiple lanes of traffic, the montage of restaurants, hotels, car lots, blinking traffic lights and strip malls.

"Only yesterday this was a small fishing village with dirt streets," he said.

"Now you have traffic gridlock and almost a million people." She tried to imagine what her passenger was experiencing, but the concept escaped her.

He twisted his neck, looking upward as they passed a bungee-jump crane amidst a group of carnival rides. "What's that?"

"People ride to the top of the crane, attach elastic ropes called bungee cords to their ankles and dive off."

"On purpose?" His voice reeked with skepticism.

She laughed. "For fun."

"Suicide—for fun?"

"They don't hit the ground. The bungee cord yanks them upward at the last minute. Most of the time."

He stared at her in disbelief.

"Remind me sometime to tell you about skydiving."

Reluctantly she pulled her gaze away from eyes like mountain mist back to the six-lane, traffic-clogged road, glad her sunglasses hid her eyes, afraid her interest might shine too visibly there.

A red and blue sign indicated the bank she'd been searching for, and she pulled into the drive-through lane.

"How much of this do you want in cash?" She endorsed his check with her name and account number.

"I don't know what things cost in your time," he admitted. "Will ten thousand buy what I need?"

She quashed a grin. "I think you can squeeze by on that. But what will you do with the rest?"

"Deposit it in your account."

"You're taking quite a chance, aren't you? I could skip back to Atlanta with your ninety thousand and leave you penniless." She searched his face, wondering at his motive. He may have been an astute businessman in his own time, but with such a trusting attitude he'd never survive the dog-eat-dog world of the present.

"You wouldn't do that."

The warmth of his tone brought a flush to her cheeks. "How can you be so sure?"

"Because you're different from any woman I've ever met. I trust you."

"Ouch," she joked, uneasy with his compliment. "That doesn't say much for the women of the 1890s."

"No, it doesn't." He thought of Selena and her fascination with his money and the power that accompanied it. The difference between Selena and Victoria Caswell was as wide as a hundred years.

He studied the woman beside him, remembering the long, slender legs and bare midriff exposed by her bathing costume when she'd returned to her suite earlier. Her trim waist above gently swelling hips was a real waist, not one artificially nipped in by torturous corsets. He pulled his gaze away and attempted to concentrate on the gaily lighted signs that lined the highway. He couldn't afford to fall in love. Selena had proved it wasn't profitable.

SEVERAL HOURS LATER, Tory massaged an aching foot as she sat at a table in the food court, watching Rand make the circuit. He'd begun with a gyro, Greek salad and a slice of pizza, while she ate frozen yogurt. Then he'd consumed a bear claw, ice cream, chocolate chip cookies and a large Coke. The man ate as if he had hollow legs.

And what legs. The trim jeans they'd purchased for him to wear while they shopped revealed the powerful muscles of his thighs and sat snugly on lean hips below his narrow waist. A striped rugby shirt hugged the contours of his muscular chest, and a London Fog windbreaker and deck shoes completed his transformation to modern fashion. Except for his astonishing good looks, he blended in perfectly with the afternoon crowd at the mall.

He settled at the table across from her, finishing the last of the cookies. "Is that all you're eating?"

"Some of us have to watch our weight." She could hate him if he hadn't been enjoying himself so conspicuously.

His gaze raked her body with an assessing eye. "You don't seem to have a problem."

"And I intend to keep it that way."

He shrugged. "Suit yourself, but I'm taking you to dinner tonight to repay you for the trouble I've been, and I expect you to make the most of it. I understand the hotel chef is one of the world's finest."

He reminded her of her father, expecting others to jump when he snapped his fingers. "How do you know about the chef?"

"Emma told me."

"Ah, the ubiquitous Emma. My life was calm and ordinary until she appeared. Since then I've encountered a ghost and a time traveler. Who knows what's next?"

He wiped his lips with a paper napkin, pushed back from the table and stood. "Do I have everything I need?"

She surveyed the mountain of packages and shopping bags that surrounded them. "Cords, more jeans, sports shirts, running shoes, dress slacks and jacket, a suit, shirts, shoes, silk ties, underwear, pajamas and robe, shaving kit, toiletries—what else is there?"

"We can always come back tomorrow." He began gathering up packages and piling them into her arms. "Now there's one very important errand to run before we return to the hotel."

She peered at him between the bags that blocked her vision. "I'll be lucky to make it as far as the car."

He relieved her of the packages that obscured her eyes, stuffing them beneath his arm before picking up a trio of shopping bags in each hand. "The next stop won't take long. I want to borrow some books on time travel from the local library."

She waited until they'd loaded their packages in the trunk and headed toward the hotel before confronting him. "The only books you'll find on time travel are in the fiction section. I told you, it isn't possible."

He turned halfway toward her before his seat belt restrained him. "I'm here, so it has to be possible. And the library should have the names of the leading authorities in the study of time. I'll contact them all if I have to, to find out how to return."

She admired his persistence but knew it wouldn't get him what he wanted. She removed one hand from the wheel and laid it on his knee in a consoling gesture. "Things aren't so bad in the 1990s. Maybe you'd better get used to them. I think you're going to be here a while."

"Not if I have any say in the matter. If there was a way to get here, there has to be a method to go back."

She jerked her hand away and struck the steering wheel. "Dammit, this isn't one of your financial deals you can force by the strength of your will. You'd better expend your efforts on finding a place to live and earning a living. You can stay with me for now, but in less than two weeks I'll be going home. Then what will you do?''

The line of his jaw hardened as if sheathed in steel. "If you don't want to drive me to the library, you can let me out here and I'll call a taxi."

She breathed deeply to control her anger, gripping the wheel as if throttling his neck. Rand Trent was without a doubt the most pigheaded man she'd ever met.

"I'll take you," she muttered between gritted teeth. "You'll need my help with the computerized cataloging systems."

"And if I find it a total waste of time, I'll buy dinner tomorrow night, as well." His low, mellow voice caressed her ears, and although she kept her eyes on the road, she could hear the smile in his words.

He was smiling still an hour later as the library printer spewed out a bibliography of several articles from scientific journals.

"There's one on time travel by Professor Christopher Smallwood at North Carolina University at Raleigh," he said. "Good place to start, don't you think?"

"If you insist on pursuing this, the little men in white coats will come and take us both away." She ripped the ribbon of tractor paper from the printer.

"Little men in white coats?"

"From the loony bin, the funny farm, the nuthouse—"

His eyes stared blankly at her, struggling to understand.

"—the insane asylum."

"I see." A worried frown replaced his former look of triumph. "We'll have to proceed carefully and not call attention to ourselves. I'm sure you'll think of a plan."

"Why me?"

"You know the current idioms, the culture. While I would take a sensible and rational approach, it might appear madness to someone of your era."

She came eye-to-eye with molten pewter and found it irresistible. Madness. That's what was happening to her. "We'll have to locate these articles first and make copies, unless you want to take the time to read them now."

"Copying several articles will take days. Won't they allow us to check out the journals?"

She grinned, feeling like Santa Claus. "You liked the computer, you're gonna love the copy machine."

She located the journals with the articles on time and began feeding dimes into the copier. He watched in fascination as the first article was reproduced, but as the tedious process continued, he wandered off.

When she had completed her copies, she went in search of Rand and found him in the nonfiction section, leaning against the stacks with one foot propped on a lower shelf, an open book in his hands.

The beauty of his face in repose, his casual posture that revealed his latent strength and the way his hair fell across his brow as he read convinced her that her instincts were on target. He was perfect for the investment firm's campaign.

"Reading more about time?" Her voice broke the quiet of the secluded aisle.

He glanced up in surprise, so absorbed in his reading he hadn't heard her approach. "No, finance."

She glanced at the title of the volume in his hands. "A history of the stock market?"

He looked like a kid caught with his hand in the cookie jar. "I thought this might come in handy when I return to where—when I belong."

"But that's cheating!" Her indignation was short-lived. The poor guy would never get the chance to use his insider information.

"I prefer thinking of it as making the best of a bad situation." He shoved the book onto the shelf, grasped her by the elbow and propelled her toward the door. "But now we must hurry to the hotel."

"What's the rush?" She attempted to fold the tractor paper trailing behind her as he tugged her toward the parking lot.

"You, Miss Caswell, have to prepare for what I believe is called 'a hot date.'"

She hid a smile as she ducked into the driver's seat. He learned fast. Which was a good thing, considering he was going to be stuck in the future for a long, long time.

THAT EVENING, Tory sipped her wine spritzer in a quiet corner of the hotel bar, shifted to a more comfortable position on the soft leather banquette and scribbled another note on the pad in front of her. Rand Trent's inspiration made her pen fly across the page. She'd left him in their room to shower and dress for dinner. When he'd finished, it would be her turn.

Through the tall windows at the other end of the room, the tropical sky had deepened to the color of mangoes following the sunset, and the gulf's smooth waters pulsed a deep teal blue. A tuxedoed pianist in the far corner coaxed soft jazz from a black, lacquered grand piano.

A deep sigh exploded in her chest. Just as well Rand wasn't there. She'd found herself drawn to the handsome time traveler, and such a setting would only amplify his appeal. The best way to resist his Victorian charm was to keep her mind on business.

"Everything working out for you, m'dear?" Emma's cheerful British voice roused her from her reverie.

"Everything?" Her mind, still focused on her Money Man, didn't grasp Emma's question.

"Your room arrangements. Has Mr. Trent settled in?" Emma whisked away the half-full glass and replaced it with a fresh drink.

"I didn't know you worked the bar." Tory laid her pen down and gazed at the elderly woman with suspicion. Every time the little maid had shown up in the past two days, she'd been a prelude to trouble.

"Just helping out Charlie." Emma nodded to the tall black man behind the bar, polishing glasses. He smiled and nodded in her direction before turning to a customer at the bar. "He's shorthanded tonight. There's a flu bug making the rounds of the staff."

"That's all I need," Tory groaned. "A strange man to share my room and influenza to boot."

"You mustn't worry. You'll be fine. Just drink your wine and relax." Emma patted her hand in a motherly gesture. "You're on vacation, remember?"

Tory glanced at the notes before her. "Looks as if this is going to be a working vacation. Would you bring me a phone, please?"

Disapproval wrinkled the maid's forehead. "Now?"

Tory motioned toward the wall behind her. "That is a phone jack, isn't it?"

Emma shrugged and scurried away, returning a moment later with a telephone. She leaned over, plugged it into the bar wall, then rose, red faced from the exertion, and confronted Tory. "Why spoil this beautiful evening with business talk? Don't you have a date for dinner?"

Tory's hand paused above the phone's buttons. "How did you know?"

But Emma was already moving away to the opposite side of the room. Tory shivered. Something was strange about the cheery little woman, but she couldn't put her finger on it. Emma seemed too kind and happy to be dangerous, and yet—she gave herself a mental shake, forcing Emma from her thoughts, and returned to the phone, punching in her credit card number, then the Atlanta number of Kristin Foster, her administrative assistant.

Kristin's perky voice with only the slightest hint of Southern drawl answered after the third ring. In the background, a television was blaring.

"Kristin, is this a bad time?" She pulled her pad closer and flipped to its front page.

"No, I just fed the kids and settled them in front of the TV. How was the wedding?"

"Great. I'll tell you all about it when I get back."

"And Florida?"

"It's great, too—"

"Meet any handsome guys?"

Tory endeavored to keep the impatience from her voice. "That's why I'm calling. I've met the perfect man for the Benson, Jurgen and Ives campaign."

"You've signed him?" Kristin half covered the receiver and yelled, "You kids stop fighting or I'll turn that off!"

"Not yet. I'm going to pitch the idea to him tonight. Meanwhile, I want you to call the writers. Have them work up a segment—"

"Hold on while I grab a pencil." The sound of drawers opening and closing crossed the wire. "Okay, shoot."

"I want a script based on the idea that making money is what he does, and he doesn't apologize for it. Also, contact the photographers and cameramen. I need a set, a Victorian office suite." She stopped long enough for Kristin to finish writing and took a long drink of the wine Emma had brought her.

"Got it. What else?" Kristin's voice seemed to come from far away.

Tory stared at the pad before her, but her eyes wouldn't focus. She couldn't concentrate. Hell, she was probably coming down with the flu Emma had mentioned.

"That's enough for now. Get started on it in the morning and I'll check in with you tomorrow." She thrust the pad away and sipped her drink again.

"Right." A child shrieked in the background. "Lucky woman, enjoy yourself."

As Tory put down the receiver, Emma appeared at her elbow. "Through with the phone, Miss Caswell?"

Her moment of giddiness had passed. She glanced at her notes with disinterest. "Yes, thanks. Take it away. I have a hot date to prepare for."

As Tory slid off the leather banquette and headed for the door, she heard Emma call her name.

"Your notepad, Miss Caswell."

She took the pad Emma offered and tucked it beneath her arm. "Thanks."

Emma's amethyst eyes twinkled as if she knew a happy secret. "Enjoy your dinner, Miss Caswell."

Tory strolled contentedly down the carpeted hallway, humming the strains from the bar's piano. When she entered her room, she tossed the notebook onto the desk. "Rand?"

The bathroom door stood open, but Rand was nowhere in sight. Lovely man. He'd probably deserted the premises to give her privacy to dress. His fresh sandalwood scent wafted on the current from the air-conditioning vent and mixed with the pleasing aroma of new leather.

She opened her closet. Her clothes hung on the left side of the expansive space. To the right, Rand's new clothes hung neatly with his running shoes and Top-Siders lined up on the floor beneath them. A feeling of satisfaction suffused her as she observed his clothes juxtaposed with hers. It seemed so . . . cozy.

Belting out a Whitney Houston love ballad, she stripped off her clothes, wrapped a terry robe around her and ran the water for her bath, adding fragrant bath salts that matched her perfume. As she slipped into the steamy water, she lay back, closed her eyes and pictured Rand with the Florida sun shining on hair the color of rich coffee and catching the gleam of a smile that cocked the right corner of his mouth.

She remembered the way the fabric of his rugby shirt pulled across the muscles of his chest, the taut fit of his jeans across his hips, the long fingers of his hands leafing through a book. Somewhere in the back of her mind, niggling thoughts of an ad campaign surfaced, only to drown again in a deluge of sensuous images.

An hour later, she stood before the full-length mirror, studying the fit of her new dress, when someone knocked at the door. She opened it to Rand, dressed in gray slacks, navy jacket and claret tie, holding out a large white box.

"For you." He entered the room and closed the door behind him.

She took the box, lifted the lid and folded back green florist paper to display two creamy white camellias tied with white satin ribbons. "A corsage! No one's given me a corsage since the senior prom."

"It is inappropriate? I'm afraid I have a great deal to learn about the customs of your time." He stood by the door, feeling he'd been punched in the stomach as he surveyed Victoria's appearance.

She wore an amazingly brief black dress, reaching several inches above the knee, with long fitted sleeves and a neckline that revealed the satiny smoothness of her tanned shoulders. A spray of shining black sequins began at her right shoulder, cascading diagonally over the formfitting garment from her firm breasts and supple hips all the way to the skirt's hem. Silky, sheer black hose encased long, slender legs, accentuated by the brevity of her skirt and high-heeled black pumps.

Fire flamed in his belly as she tilted her head toward him, bathing him with the glow of her sea green eyes. "Flowers are always appropriate. They're lovely."

She stood before the mirror, placing the corsage first on one shoulder, then the other.

He moved behind her. Her magnolia fragrance encompassed him as he raised a hand to her hair, shining like burnished gold, which she'd arranged in a chignon that exposed the slender column of her neck.

"Wear them here," he suggested, touching her hair.

Selena would have fastened them to her bodice, just to be perverse, but Victoria placed the flowers where he'd pointed and secured them with hairpins.

His hands brushed her bare shoulders. "I've reserved a table on the terrace. You won't be too cool there?"

She crossed to the dresser and drew a black cashmere stole from the bottom drawer. "I'll be fine. But surely you're not hungry after all you ate at the mall?"

"Ravenous," he assured her, but his hunger wasn't centered in his stomach.

BEYOND the soft lights of the terrace the moon hung low over the tranquil gulf, flanked by two bright stars. A cool breeze, laden with a tropical perfume, wafted across their table.

"Mmm." Tory took a deep breath. "Orange blossoms."

"Where's that scent coming from? Where the groves used to be, there's nothing but houses and shops." Rand stared off into the darkness across the golf course that bordered the hotel on the east and south.

"People here grow oranges and grapefruit in their yards, much as we do peaches and pears in Atlanta." She sipped her wine and appraised the attractive man across from her. "What was it like here a hundred years ago?"

"This terrace wasn't here. Just a broad veranda and stairs leading down past the rose gardens to the railway."

"A railway? Like a train station?" She tried to imagine trains lumbering past the hotel while the guests attempted to sleep.

"A spur line, where guests who arrived in their private cars could park them during their stay."

"Did you have your own car?" Her interest in his life in the Gay Nineties escalated.

"I traveled to Florida in my own railcar, but I stayed in the hotel once I sent my car back to Chicago." He rolled the tulip glass between his palms, drawing her gaze to the study squareness of his hands.

"To pick up someone?" A surge of jealousy nipped her from out of nowhere.

He shook his head. "To take someone home—but that's a long, unpleasant story I'd rather not go into."

His hint of mystery quickened her interest. "Tell me about yourself then."

He shrugged self-effacingly. "There's not much to tell. My father made his fortune supplying the army during the war—the Civil War. We moved into the big house on Lake Shore Drive in Chicago when I was still a toddler."

"And your parents?" she prompted.

The lines of his jaw hardened. "Drowned in a boating accident on Lake Michigan a few years later. I was reared by my bachelor uncle, a rather grim man, whose main interest in life was making money. He taught me to preserve and multiply my father's wealth."

A discreet cough at her elbow announced the waiter's return. Rand ordered for the two of them, while his comment about wealth rattled around in the fog in her brain, a niggling reminder of something she couldn't identify.

She should never have had that second spritzer; she hadn't been able to think straight since. Yet there she was, drinking vintage champagne as if she knew what she was doing, so relaxed she uttered the next words that rolled into her head.

"You must have been a very sad little boy."

His eyes darkened as he tossed back the last of his champagne. "Yes, I suppose I was."

She watched the pain flitting through the depth of his eyes, turning their pale gray smoke to granite. His uncle had taught him about money. Had anyone taught him about love?

"And were you a happy little girl?"

His unexpected question flooded her with nostalgia, remembrances of Jill and her, bundling into their matching coats on a cold winter morning for the ride to school. Then picnics for their dolls among the crepe myrtles on a sultry summer afternoon, her father taking endless pictures beneath the tree on Christmas Eve, her mother baking peanut butter cookies on a Saturday morning.

She smiled at his through a haze of tears. "Oh, yes. I had a wonderful childhood. My parents are both gone now. And Jill's with her husband in Australia. But I'm thankful for my memories."

He reached across the damask cloth and clasped her hand. She welcomed the warmth of his grasp. The pain vanished from his eyes as he smiled at her, and the line of his jaw softened. She studied his tanned face with its pleasing planes, strong brow and patrician nose, features any woman would admire—and in the back attics of her memory, a thought rattled at the door, trying unsuccessfully to escape.

The arrival of the waiter, who assembled their Caesar salad beside their table, stilled the insistent clamoring in her head.

Over poached salmon with dill sauce, fresh asparagus and new potatoes, accompanied by a dry white wine, she plied him with questions about the hotel's past.

"The man who built the Bellevue was a genius at making money," Rand said, as if bestowing his highest form of praise. "He'd built a railroad down the west coast into the Tampa Bay area, and to encourage visitors to use it, he constructed two large resorts, one here at Clearwater Harbor, the other across the bay at Tampa."

"But how did they stand the summer heat, especially before air-conditioning? People wore so many layers of clothing then." She appreciated scorching summers. Atlanta was famous for them.

He took a bite of salmon and chewed thoughtfully, his appetite apparently undiminished by his earlier raid on the mall's food court. "The hotel was only open from right after Christmas until just before Easter. But most guests stayed the whole time, paying a price dear enough to justify closing the remainder of the year."

No matter how she steered the conversation, he always came back to money. *Money Man.* Where had the phrase come from?

"Lovely night, isn't it?" Emma appeared at their table, filling Tory's coffee cup from a silver pot.

"Don't you ever rest?" The little woman was beginning to get on her nerves. "You've been here since morning."

"As I said, there's influenza among the staff. The rest of us are doubling up." She moved to Rand's place, pouring the aromatic brew into his cup, as well. "Having dessert, Mr. Trent?"

"How could I resist fresh strawberry shortcake?"

"Enjoy your evening, m'dears." Emma moved away and Tory sighed with relief, knowing the woman made her nervous but not understanding why.

Rank took another swallow of coffee. "I have a request to make of you. It's very—" His mind went totally blank. Where had his thought gone?

He forgot his vanished question as the waiter placed a dish, heaped with strawberries, cake and mounds of whipped cream, in front of him. He took a large bite and his expression dissolved into a look of pure pleasure.

Whipped cream melted on his tongue and the flavor of strawberries burst upon his palate. "Are you sure you won't try this?"

"I couldn't eat another bite."

He dug into the rich dessert once more, but his appetite inexplicably disappeared. He set down his spoon and shoved the dish aside.

Across the table, Victoria's eyes shimmered like a cloudless sky, her shoulders glowed with the creamy translucence of magnolia blossoms, her scent teased his nostrils.

"The evening's too beautiful to waste." He pushed back his chair. "Let's take a walk in the moonlight."

When she stood, he draped her shawl around her shoulders, fighting the urge to enfold her in his arms.

"A wonderful idea." Her voice, low and melodious, caressed him like a song.

He drew her arm through his and led her down the terrace steps to the drive that circled the hotel. The southern breeze, warm and scented with citrus blossoms, lifted tendrils of her hair off her forehead. When they reached the shadows beneath a towering pine, he pulled her into his arms. The heat of her body pulsed beneath his fingertips, causing a responding flare deep within him.

"Victoria . . ."

He felt her stiffen beneath his touch and a corresponding chill filled the breeze. Her eyes, staring wildly at a point past his shoulder, refused to meet his. He pivoted, forcing her behind him, between him and whatever had frightened her.

Glowing with a strange light in the deep shadows, Angelina Fairchild approached, her turquoise gown and midnight black curls whipping frantically in the suddenly still air.

He heard the sharp intake of her breath as she raised the back of one hand to her lips.

"You!" she gasped. And vanished in the night air.

Chapter Five

A cloud trailed across the moon, casting a deeper pall to the shadows. Then the plaintive call of a whippoorwill and the scurrying of dry leaves across the drive broke the eerie silence Angelina had left in her wake.

Tory clasped Rand's arm for support, afraid her trembling knees would buckle on her. "Did you see her?"

Even in the deep shadows, his face paled visibly beneath his tan as he turned to her and pulled her shuddering body against the hard muscles of his chest.

"I saw."

He held her close and the steady beat of his heart beneath his smooth linen shirt, pulsating against her cheek, reassured her. She snuggled deeper into his embrace, savoring the confidence his nearness created, the *rightness* of his arms around her.

After a few minutes, she pulled away, disconcerted by her response to him, smoothing her tousled hair from her face. She tugged her shawl tightly around her, unable to shake the cold Angelina's presence had driven to her body's core.

"Let's go inside." Her voice wavered, echoing her inner turmoil.

Rand grasped her elbow, and they plodded silently to their room. The moon shone dully, and the magic had disappeared from the night.

IN THEIR SUITE, Rand sat on the sofa, staring into nothingness. He'd removed his coat and tie and loosened the top button of his shirt. His face, void of expression, settled into stern lines.

Plunging his hand into his pocket, he withdrew it empty. "I forgot about my watch. What time is it?"

She glanced at the digital clock beside her bed. "After eleven."

He groaned. "Too late for room service, and I could really use a drink."

Tory opened the door of the minibar beside the dresser. "Name your poison."

"Scotch." He raked long fingers through his thick hair, then accepted the glass of Chivas Regal with a mumbled thanks. Tipping back the glass, he downed the liquor in a gulp.

"What's going on around here?" His hand trembled slightly as he lowered the glass to the coffee table.

Sitting in the chair across from him with her feet tucked beneath her, she remembered Angelina's hand on Rand's arm in the picture in the west hallway. "You tell me."

His brows arched questioningly.

"You're the one who appeared in my room after my first encounter with Angelina. You're the one she recognized tonight. So what gives?"

He flung his arms wide along the back of the sofa, leaned his head on the backrest and stared at the ceiling. "I have no idea. I wouldn't be surprised right now to see pigs fly."

Exhaustion seeped from her every pore. The past twenty-four hours had been an emotional roller coaster ride from terror to pleasure and excitement, then back to terror again,. Her body cried out for sleep, but her mind wouldn't rest until she had some answers. "Are you the man Angelina is looking for?"

With a heavy sigh, he leaned forward, cradling his head in his hands. Whatever the day had been for her, she knew he'd been through worse.

"Am I the lover with whom she quarreled? No. Did she recognize me? Of course. The hotel was a third this size—yesterday." He grimaced at the irony of the word. "All the guests were acquainted with one another."

"Emma said Angelina appears only to brides here. But Jill didn't see her. She would have told me. And now Angelina's approached me twice. I don't get it."

Her weariness mirrored his own. He dragged himself from the sofa's depths, then lifted her by her elbows to her feet. "You must be exhausted. Why don't you retire now? We can sort this out in the morning."

She nodded in agreement. Groggy with fatigue, she wandered into the bathroom, stripped off her dress and stockings, tugged on a warm gown and fleecy robe and thrust her feet into fuzzy slippers.

When she emerged from the bathroom, Rand gathered her in his arms. She sagged for a moment against him, wanting to take comfort again in his embrace but knowing it wasn't a good idea. She drew away, tilting her face toward him, smiling to ease her rebuff.

"Thank you for the lovely dinner. I'm sorry Angelina spoiled its ending."

He lifted a honeyed curl off her forehead and brushed her smooth skin with his lips. The taste of her sent a river of fire coursing through his veins and he had to rally all his better instincts to keep from crushing her to him.

Of all that had happened to him, the surge of unfamiliar tenderness the woman caused in him was the strangest occurrence of all.

With reluctance, he stepped away. "Sleep well, Victoria."

She smiled at him. "I don't know if I can, after all that's happened."

But when he came out of the bathroom after changing into his nightclothes, she lay fast asleep in the middle of the large double bed.

She had unfolded the sofa and turned down the covers for him. Rand slipped between the sheets, fearing, for all his exhaustion, sleep would elude him. But the steady, even whisper of Victoria's breathing soon lulled him into slumber.

A MOCKINGBIRD warbled a small symphony in the cypress tree outside her window. Tory turned onto her stomach and dragged a pillow over her head to block the brilliant sun, thankful she didn't have to report to the office.

The office!

She bolted upright and threw back the covers, reaching for her robe. She had assured Kristin she'd sign Rand as spokesperson for the project, but she'd totally forgotten the Money Man campaign while she was with him last night. What was the matter with her?

She stopped short at the sight of Rand, sleeping soundly, sprawled across the sofa bed with the covers kicked down around his ankles. He wore only the bottom of a pair of midnight blue silk pajamas and the sight of his bare, muscled torso squeezed the air from her lungs.

She congratulated herself at the picture he presented. Her idea had been nothing short of brilliant. If every woman who viewed a Money Man ad featuring Randolph Trent had the same reaction as hers, Benson, Jurgen and Ives would be beating off female investors with a stick, and Caswell & Associates would cement its status as the most successful advertising agency in the Southeast.

Rand rolled onto his back, brushing a shock of hazel hair off his face. When he opened his eyes and saw her, he smiled languidly, sending waves of heat washing over her, accompanied by an affection that brought a tightness to her chest.

"Good morning." His pleasing baritone strummed every nerve in her body, and the sensation alarmed her.

"Did you sleep all right on that thing?" She nodded toward the sofa bed.

"As if I'd been drugged." He sat on its edge and stretched, sending intoxicating ripples across his chest and down his biceps.

She pulled her gaze away. She'd have to be careful, working with such a gorgeous guy. Falling in love would add unwanted complications to her life.

She had to find a way to douse the heat he ignited in her. "I'm going for a swim. Want to come?"

SHE DIVED into the large pool of the indoor spa and began swimming laps. She'd logged only two lengths before Rand, dressed in the Speedo bikini the spa attendant had provided, plunged in beside her. So much for taking her mind off his handsome physique. His abbreviated suit molded around his groin and buttocks like plastic wrap, leaving nothing to her imagination, which proceeded to run amok at the sight.

She plunged her face into the cool water, churning its surface with a determined breaststroke. She had to get a grip. The man was business, nothing more.

After her requisite number of laps, she levered herself onto the side of the pool and wrapped herself in a giant towel. Reclining in a folding chair beneath the wide skylight, she ordered orange juice.

For once, Emma was nowhere in sight.

Rand joined her, his towel wrapped around his waist. He folded himself onto the chair beside her, then stretched long, firm legs before him. "Of all the differences between your century and mine, the custom of the sexes mingling company in the briefest of attire is the most difficult to adjust to."

"Sometimes I have trouble with it myself," she muttered into her orange juice, averting her eyes from the man at her side. "You didn't have all this exercise equipment in your day, and jogging wasn't fashionable. How did you manage to stay in such good condition?"

"Riding is my favorite form of exercise."

Her dream of him cantering up the avenue from the hotel's entrance filled her head. Strange she should have dreamed of him at almost the instant he'd stepped through time. But then what hadn't been strange about the past forty-eight hours?

He spoke briefly to the attendant who'd approached him, then turned to her. "Would you like to ride with me this afternoon?"

She shook her head.

Disappointment covered his face. "You don't ride?"

"I've ridden before, but not here. The hotel's stables are long gone."

He sighed, whipped the towel from his waist and began to rub his hair dry. "About last night—"

"We need to talk—" They'd both spoken at once, and she nodded for him to continue. He could have his say, then she'd pitch the Money Man idea to him.

"I have to return to my time before the end of the week or the most important negotiations of my career will collapse."

She bit back an angry reply. "I told you, you *can't* go back. You might as well get used to the fact. Besides, even if you could return, how do you know you'd go back to the same time and place?"

"I'll have to take that chance. I have millions at stake." He smiled. "Believe me, I understand your skepticism. The majority of people share it."

"You've talked to others about this?" She'd have to stick closer to him or he'd end up in the loony bin for sure.

He shook his head, spraying droplets of water. "While you dressed for dinner last night, I read the articles on time we found at the library."

Her lips tightened in a stubborn line. "Then you must know I'm right. You can't go back."

"Dr. Christopher Smallwood isn't quite as certain as you."

The spa attendant returned. "Your orange juice, sir, and today's *Wall Street Journal.*"

She raised an eyebrow at the newspaper. "Some light reading?"

"Since I'm here I might as well try a few investments."

"Don't you ever think of anything but money?" she grumbled. His penchant for investment—plus his incredible good looks—made him perfect for her advertising campaign. So why was she complaining?

"Yes. Right now I'm thinking about how to return where I belong."

They were going around in circles. She attempted to break the cycle. "I have a proposition for you."

A wicked grin cocked the corner of his wide mouth. "It's been a long time since I was propositioned by a lovely lady in dishabille."

"That's not the kind of proposition I meant." A flush crept over her, destroying the cooling effect of her swim. "A business proposition."

Shrewdness replaced the warmth in his eyes. "What kind of business?"

"I own an advertising agency back in Atlanta—"

"You?"

She smiled at his expression of shocked disbelief. "Women do have their own businesses now, and one of my newest clients is Benson, Jurgen and Ives."

"The investment firm?"

She nodded.

"I've corresponded with them." He looked thoughtful. "They're a new firm but with a very impressive record."

His interest sent a thrill of triumph through her. "Not new anymore. They celebrated their centennial five years ago. Their company motto stresses over a hundred years of satisfied clients. That's where you come in."

"Me?" He choked on his orange juice. "What do I have to do with them? I conduct my own brokering out of Chicago."

"Not in the last hundred years," she reminded him gently.

"I don't understand. Are you asking me to work for them?"

"In a manner of speaking. Actually, I'm asking you to work for me." She held her breath, waiting for his reply.

His expression turned wary. "Doing what?"

She mentally crossed her fingers and plunged ahead. "Acting as spokesman for the Money Man campaign I'm planning for Benson, Jurgen and Ives."

"Money Man?"

"Part of the pitch for their advertising. You inspired me. 'Making money is what I do. I don't apologize for it.'" She glimpsed the flicker of rekindled curiosity in his granite eyes. "You'd be featured in both print and television ads."

His frown sent her hopes plummeting. "Sounds undignified. Besides, I don't plan to be here that long."

Ignoring his last words, Tory focused on the first. "The ads would be very tasteful. Split page and split screen. You as the reserved, prosperous broker of the 1890s on one side, and on the other, as the reliable investor of the 1990s. You'd represent one hundred years of continual, dependable service."

"But why me?" His brow wrinkled in a puzzled scowl.

"We call it typecasting. You look like a reliable investment broker, you talk like one, therefore, in the minds of the public, you—representative of Benson, Jurgen and Ives—must *be* a reliable broker.''

And every female investor in America will fall madly in love with you, she added silently, *and beat a path to my client's door.*

''It's a clever idea but, as I said, I won't be here long enough to help you. Professor Smallwood believes time travel is possible.''

Her eyes widened with skepticism. ''You're kidding. A scientist of his caliber?'' Then another thought struck her. If Smallwood was right, she might never see Rand Trent again. The thought hung like a gray cloud in the back of her mind.

He sat on the side of the chaise, his strong hands clasped between his knees. ''Smallwood's a man of impeccable credentials. And his theories are exciting.''

''Aha! So we're still speaking theoretically here.'' Smugness dripped from her voice.

He thrust a bare, lean arm toward her. ''Pinch me.''

''Why?''

''Just do it.''

The stern look in his eyes compelled her to do as he said. She reached forward and grasped his muscled forearm between the pads of two fingers. The feel of him set her nerve ends tingling, and she pulled her hand back. She had to clear her throat of the emotion that clogged it before she could speak.

''So?'' she croaked, still quivering from the nearness of him.

"So there's nothing theoretical about *me*. I'm here, flesh and blood, living proof that time travel can happen."

He was flesh and blood, all right, and driving her senses wild. She struggled to focus on the issue at hand. "But your being here is some sort of fluke. You don't really expect Dr. Smallwood to replicate that accident and send you back?"

His lips lifted in an engaging grin that sent her humming senses into overdrive. "Read his article when we get to the room. You'll see he's on to something."

Pity for him stabbed through her. If she was in his place, she supposed she'd grasp at any straw to return where she belonged.

Rand read the skepticism on her face. He'd negotiated with skeptics before—and won. "Now I have a proposition for you. A bit of quid pro quo."

Her seawater eyes shone in the soft morning sun filtering through the skylight above the pool. "I'm listening."

"You arrange a meeting for me with Dr. Smallwood and accompany me to Raleigh. If he convinces us both it's impossible to send me back to my time, then I'll be your Money Man."

Triumph flashed across her delicate features, and she proffered him a slender hand. "Mr. Trent, you have yourself a deal."

Disappointment flooded him. Selena had loved him for his money, had left him when it wasn't enough. Now Victoria wanted to use him to make money for herself.

He walled off the tenderness he'd begun to feel toward her. Everything in life, after all, was only business.

He shook her hand to seal the agreement, wondering why, if it was only business, he found himself so reluctant to release her.

He stood and pulled her to her feet. "Let's get started."

She stared at him, openmouthed for a second, then clamped her jaw shut and walked toward the spa exit. He followed on her heels. She was in a hurry to prove him wrong, but her haste would work to his advantage. Jason Phiswick had promised him an answer on his stock proposal by the weekend, and Rand intended to be there to hear it.

WHILE VICTORIA SHOWERED and dressed, Rand re-read Smallwood's article. The scientific jargon made comprehension difficult, but if the scientist proposed what Rand thought, he could soon kiss the twentieth century goodbye.

Absently, he picked up her black cashmere shawl lying across the desk chair and held its softness against his face. The scent of magnolias enveloped him and a spasm of loss twisted his heart. He tossed the shawl across the chair, raked his fingers through his damp hair and tried to force Tory from his mind. Selena's cruelty, only a few weeks old, still festered, reminding him to stick to business, which he understood, and avoid the perplexities of the female sex.

OVER A BREAKFAST of fresh fruit, yogurt and English muffins delivered by room service, Tory reiterated her reservations about Dr. Smallwood. "To keep their tenure, university professors have to publish in professional journals on a regular basis. Often *what* they write isn't as important as the fact that it's been published. Maybe the article was meant as an inside joke among physicists."

Rand polished off his third muffin, heaped with strawberry jam. "I don't think so. It's a complex theory, but if I understand it correctly, Smallwood contends that time folds back onto itself and occasionally two separate points on the time continuum intersect—"

"Sounds good for 'Star Trek,' but I don't buy it."

"Star trek?"

"A television show about the exploration of the universe. One of my favorites, actually."

"Is there such a thing?"

"Star travel?" She poured herself more coffee and stirred it absently. "No, manned flights have only gone as far as the moon."

Frustration gleamed in his eyes. "You can believe men travel to the moon, but you can't accept Smallwood's theory?"

"I *saw* the moon flight films. Nobody's ever seen time travelers." She leaned back in her chair, pleased to have made her point.

"Except you," he said with a knowing grin.

Morning sun illuminated his face, accentuating a profile so handsome it was dangerous. The smile he threw her turned her stomach into a hyperactive gymnast.

"How do you know," he asked, "that there aren't hundreds, even thousands of others like me, who appear perfectly normal, but have adopted the manners and dress of your time in order to blend in?"

She opened her mouth, hoping to rebut him, but her brain went blank.

He reached across the table and covered her hand with his. "Time must have folded back on itself here in this room the night I appeared in your bed. That's why I have to see Smallwood, to see if there's a chance it will happen again."

She caught the glitter of excitement in his eyes. He had placed his hopes in Smallwood, but she feared he was setting himself up for disappointment.

After wiping his lips with his napkin, he tossed it onto his empty plate. "When do we start?"

"We don't even know if Smallwood will see us."

He squeezed her hand. "When we tell him what happened to me—"

"He'll dismiss you as a certifiable nut case and refuse further calls." She pulled her hands away from the deliciously comfortable feel of his flesh against her own.

"Maybe not."

And if Smallwood *did* believe that Rand had traveled through time? She pictured a media circus with intrusive microphones, rolling cameras, popping flash-bulbs and glaring tabloid headlines, all portraying Rand as some kind of freak. With his image and credibility in shreds, she could forget her Money Man campaign.

"We can't take the chance of his refusing to believe you," she insisted. "We won't tell him you're from the past."

He stood and shoved his hands into the back pockets of his jeans in frustration. "How can I ask what I need to know without telling him what's happened?"

"We make something up."

"You mean *lie* to Smallwood?" His face darkened with outraged integrity.

"No, we won't lie—at least, not exactly." She fidgeted under the intensity of his gaze. "We have to find a way of telling him *without* telling him."

He slumped onto the couch, propped his running shoes on the coffee table and clasped his hands behind his head. His laser stare never left her face. "A lie of omission is still a lie."

She grinned as an idea flashed into her head. "Not a lie. Fiction."

"Like Mark Twain's *Connecticut Yankee in King Arthur's Court*?" His handsome features relaxed into a grin. "I could pretend to be a writer, working on a story about a man who wakes up in another century. I'll ask Smallwood how to return my character to his own time in a way as close to reality as possible."

Thoughts flitted through her mind like a squadron of hummingbirds. Nothing must tarnish the image or reputation of her future Money Man. She considered their visit to Smallwood a waste of time but necessary for the deal she'd made—and for Rand's sake. The only positive result she expected was his ultimate acceptance of being stuck in the twentieth century for the duration.

"We'll need credentials," she said, "to convince him to give us an appointment."

"What kind of credentials?"

"Something he can check if he wants proof that we're legitimate." She tapped a finger against her lips, thinking.

He shrugged and smiled. "That leaves me out. Officially, I'm dead, remember?"

She snapped her fingers as an idea struck her. "We'll say you're a screenwriter—"

"Screenwriter?"

"Someone who writes the stories for moving pictures. We'll tell Smallwood that Caswell & Associates are willing to underwrite the production costs of your movie. I'll give Smallwood my office number if he wants to verify my identity. Then we'll tell him you need his help in working the bugs out of the plot."

His dark brows pulled together in a frown. "Bugs?"

"Problems. We'll tell him you have to make the plot seem real—believable."

"I don't know that *I* believe any of this. How will I convince Smallwood?"

Her gaze traveled over his tall frame, from the clean-cut lines of his handsome face to the wide expanse of his chest, to narrow hips and down long, powerful legs. He had honesty and integrity stamped on every inch of him. The same virtues that made him perfect for her ad campaign, the same virtues that drew her to him in a way that thrilled and frightened her, would serve him well with Smallwood. "You'll do fine."

She picked up the phone, requested Smallwood's number from information, then placed the call.

Rand studied her as she spoke with the professor, impressed by her polished demeanor. The fiction fell smoothly from her lips, reminding him again of Selena. Were all women the schemers his former fiancée had been? But Selena's schemes had hurt him; Victoria was only trying to help.

Dressed in a short-sleeved blouse and brief, divided skirt the color of peaches, she perched on the edge of the desk, swinging one sandaled foot. The sight of her trim, tanned ankles captivated him. He tore his gaze away, reminding himself that if he got his wish, in a few more days Victoria Caswell wouldn't have been born yet.

She hung up the phone. "It's all set. He'll see us tomorrow morning at eleven."

He experienced a curious mixture of excitement at the prospect of returning home and regret for the opportunity he'd miss of knowing her better. "How do we get there?"

"We'll take my car. I'm checking out anyway, so we can return to Atlanta from Raleigh, and I'll have—"

"No."

"No?" She stared at him as if he'd lost his mind. "What do you mean, no? I thought you wanted to go to Raleigh."

"I do, but we must keep this room. This is where time changed. If I'm going to return to my own time and place, I have a feeling I'll have to do it from here."

She shook her head sadly. "You can't count on Smallwood's abilities to send you back."

"I have to try. He's the only hope I have."

A knock sounded at the door and Emma appeared to retrieve their breakfast dishes.

"Lovely day," she chirped. "The kitchen will pack you a picnic basket if you'd like to spend it on the beach."

The little maid reminded Tory of the ghost's reappearance the previous night. "Emma, tell me what you know about Angelina Fairchild."

"Angelina? Only what I already told you." She scooped the dishes into her cart and beamed at Rand. "You have a fine appetite, Mr. Trent."

"We saw her again last night on the road by the golf course," Tory said.

"Who?"

Tory prayed for patience. The woman's brain was probably tired from the long hours she'd worked. "Angelina."

Emma pushed her cart toward the door. "Very unusual. Up till now, she's only appeared to brides, never to anyone twice—" she stopped and threw a penetrating look at Rand "—and *never* to a man."

"What do you suppose she wants with me?" Tory asked.

Emma shoved the cart out the doorway and turned to Tory with an enigmatic smile. "Why don't you ask her?"

Emma closed the door, leaving Tory feeling foolish. Why had she thought the maid would know anything more about Angelina? She withdrew her suitcase from the closet and began packing clothes for the trip to Raleigh. At least once they'd left the Bellevue, she wouldn't have to worry about Angelina's ghost.

BY TEN O'CLOCK, they had crossed the causeway that spanned the bay, heading for Tampa and the interstate. Tory had loaned Rand a suitcase, and after a stop at one of the hotel shops to purchase him a pair of aviator sunglasses, they'd loaded their luggage into the trunk of her Toyota and headed north.

Seeing the world through Rand's eyes, she developed a new appreciation for jet skis on the bay waters, wide jumbo jets taking off from Tampa International Airport and complex cloverleaf interchanges on the highway. She marveled with him over the glass-faced skyscrapers of downtown Tampa and pointed out the minarets of the University of Tampa, once the Tampa Bay Hotel, built in the 1880s.

"Intriguing," he said. "I must visit there next winter."

She humored his belief that he'd return to his own time. "Don't count on it. By 1898, that hotel will be crawling with Teddy Roosevelt's Rough Riders, bound for war in Cuba."

When they left Tampa, the highway scenery became more mundane—pastures, pine forests and rolling hills blanketed with orange groves. Rand turned his attention to the digital radio, flipping from one country music station to the next.

"Amazing." He hummed along with the conclusion of a Reba McEntire tune. "Such pathos."

She snorted. Country music ranked last on her list of favorites. "There's nothing to it. You just sing through your nose about mending your broken heart, calling your coon hound and driving off into the rainy night in your pickup truck to live miserably ever after."

"But that insistent rhythm gets into your blood." Keeping time with Billy Ray Cyrus, he tapped long fingers against the skintight jeans that encased his thigh. "The lyrics hold nothing back. All the emotions are there—heartache, pain, hopes, disappointments, love. It's unreserved and straightforward."

Her blood sang, but her response had nothing to do with Billy Ray's sultry singing. The sight of Rand's fingers rapping on his thighs made it difficult for her to pay attention to her driving. Like Rand, she wanted to reach Raleigh as soon as possible, but for different reasons. The sooner she could put this wild-goose chase behind them, the sooner they could begin the Money Man campaign. The sooner he accepted he was here to stay.

The sooner he might view her as more than his guide to the twentieth century. She blinked, wondering where that last thought had popped up from.

"Won't you miss all these wonders and conveniences," she asked, "the music, the inventions, if Smallwood figures out how to send you home?"

He stopped drumming his fingers and laid a hand on her arm. "I'll miss you, Victoria. I appreciate all you've done for me."

She swallowed hard to dislodge the knot in her throat. She'd known him just over twenty-four hours and his presence had filled her unremarkable life with fun and excitement, something to look forward to besides the familiar routine of work. She tried to banish her fanciful thoughts—foolish thoughts for an independent woman.

"I'd have done the same for anyone," she lied, knowing something in his face, his manner, had drawn her to him from the beginning, preventing her from leaving him to the authorities.

The slight pressure of his hand on her arm sent a wave of pleasure rushing through her. "Come back with me, Victoria. Let me show you your world before it was trampled by too many people and millions of machines."

She laughed nervously, alarmed at the way her spirits soared at his request. But his invitation was hypothetical. She couldn't accompany him to the 1890s, because he wasn't going anywhere, except to Raleigh and then back to Atlanta with her.

She passed over his request with a chuckle. "Thanks for the invitation, but I'm a modern girl. I'd shrivel up and die without my blow dryer and microwave."

"Blow dryer? Microwave? I don't know these things."

"Modern conveniences for drying hair and cooking quickly."

"And these are important to you?" He withdrew his hand, and she returned her attention to the road.

They continued north on Interstate 75 to the accompaniment of the radio's honky-tonk beat. At Ocala, she exited and drove into a McDonald's parking lot.

"Hungry?" She didn't know why she asked. Rand's appetite never slackened.

"Won't this slow us down?" He stretched as he got out of the car, molding the smooth fabric of his knit shirt to the hard muscles of his chest and upper arms, unwittingly drawing the appreciative gaze of two teenage girls in a nearby car.

"We'll be in and out in minutes."

But when they stepped in line behind a dozen longhaired, tattooed bikers in black leather and chains, she wondered if she'd spoken too soon.

FIFTEEN MINUTES LATER they sat at a corner table. Tory nibbled her chicken salad and watched Rand consume two Big Macs, fries and a chocolate shake, reminding herself no one worried about cholesterol in the 1890s.

Watching him, she considered the Benson, Jurgen and Ives campaign. He would knock 'em dead as the Money Man with his classic good looks, cultured voice, remarkable build and those intense gray eyes flecked with silver. Every woman would love him.

But do you want to share him with every woman? an inner voice taunted her.

He interrupted her reverie. "What a marvelous idea."

"What?" She flushed, remembering her thoughts.

"Instantaneous food, uniform menus and prices. Quick and convenient for travelers. If I was going to be here longer, I'd invest in such a place."

Money again. The man was obsessed with it. "Someone else has already made his fortune off this idea."

"It obviously appeals to every element of society." He nodded toward the bikers, clustered around tables on the opposite side of the restaurant. Their raucous laughter drowned out the buzz of other voices in the noisy room. "Who are they?"

A tall man, who appeared to be the leader of the group, dropped French fries one by one into the gaping mouth of the woman next to him. His wiry black hair and beard exploded in a tortured cloud around his face, giving him the look of a victim of electric shock. His barrel chest, matted with more dark hair, was only partially covered by a leather vest, laced loosely across the front with a heavy silver chain. Tight black jeans enveloped his heavy thighs like sausage casings.

As he held a French fry above the garish lips of his bleached-blond partner, sunlight gleamed on metal studs protruding from the knuckles of his black leather gloves and animated the dragon tattoo on his bare biceps. The others of his group dressed in variations of the same theme.

"They're probably Hell's Angels," Tory explained.

"You mean *devils?*"

She laughed. "Some law enforcement officials would say so."

"But what do they do?"

"I don't know much about them, except what I've seen on television and in the movies. They're a nomadic group, traveling across the country on powerful motorcycles, sometimes finding themselves on the wrong side of the law."

"Like Gypsies."

"I suppose you could say that." The fascination in his expression made her uneasy, and his scrutiny of the group threatened to attract their attention. She attempted to divert him by pushing her untouched packet of French fries across to him.

He picked up a sliver of potato and munched contentedly, apparently forgetting the bikers.

"You haven't told me much about yourself," she said. "You make money, you ride horses. How else do you spend your time?"

He shrugged. "Work. What else is there?"

"Hobbies? Recreation?"

He looked puzzled, as if he didn't know the meaning of the words. "Sometimes I attend dinners and parties at the homes of business associates."

"And what do you do there, besides eat?"

"We talk business."

"Aha!"

He lifted his eyebrows. "Aha?"

She leaned back in her chair, folded her arms under her chest and gloated. "It's just as I thought. You don't know how to have fun."

"My uncle always frowned on frivolity. But you, I take it, had no such restrictions." He finished the last of her fries and tossed the empty packet among the discarded containers on his tray. "Enlighten me. What frivolous activities do you pursue?"

She held up her fingers and began to count. "There's—"

"Yes?" His eyes encouraged her.

She cast about in her memory but could think of nothing but work. In the year since her parents' deaths, she'd buried herself in the operation of Caswell & Associates to the exclusion of all else. No parties, no dates. Nothing but early morning jogs and long days that stretched into night at the office. Her life was as devoid of enjoyable recreation as that of the money machine across from her. She saw herself reflected in the driven man who watched her, and the similarity frightened her.

"I used to garden with my mother, before she died." Memories of red Georgia clay, peonies and roses and her mother clipping flowers for the house drowned her in waves of nostalgia. "And Jill and I used to meet our friends at a different restaurant every week before taking in a movie or a concert."

"And now?" He'd turned the tables on her with his question.

She squirmed beneath the inquisition of his gaze. "I was on vacation when I met you, remember?"

"This Money Man campaign. Do you find it relaxing?"

"No." Exhilarating, challenging, provocative, but not relaxing.

Sadness tinged his smile. "Then it's best I go back where I belong, so you can resume your holiday and enjoy the relaxation you value so highly."

His insight made her uncomfortable. She'd tried to grill him on his habits and he'd turned the spotlight on her. She didn't like what he'd shown her. A life devoid of friends and pleasure, filled only with work and obligations. What was she running from?

Commitment, her inner voice whispered, but she refused to listen. She scooted out of her chair.

"There's a pay phone at the back of the restaurant. I'll put in a call to Nellie, my housekeeper, to have the place ready for us this evening. Then I'll meet you at the car."

Without waiting for his reply, she picked up her tray, dumped her trash in the container by the door and headed for the pay phone.

TORY SQUINTED in the sunlight, donning her sunglasses as she walked toward her car. Rand was nowhere in sight.

The roar of motorcycles throttling up drew her attention to the far side of the lot, where sunlight bounced off the chrome of a dozen huge machines. The leather-clad men, intimidating with their bandannas, chains and tattoos, leaned back on their machines, revving up their engines. Riding two abreast as they exited the lot, they pulled into formation.

As the last pair drove past her, Rand peered around the massive bulk of one of the drivers, waving a cheerful farewell as the bikers roared onto the highway. In seconds they were out of sight, leaving Tory alone, staring at the cloud of dust swirling in their wake.

Chapter Six

He hadn't even said goodbye. Tory stared for several long minutes down the narrow country road where Rand and the bikers had disappeared, then climbed into her car.

"Damn!"

She slammed the heel of her hand against the steering wheel. She'd seen how the bikers intrigued him. Why hadn't she warned him to stay clear of them? Most bikers were just out for fun and relaxation, but the possibility that this rough-looking crowd was up to no good gnawed at her. She shuddered as she considered where they might take him, what they might do. He carried several thousand dollars and he was clueless about modern culture. Would they steal his money and leave him in a ditch to die?

She climbed out of the car, debating whether to call the police. Rand was a grown man. He hadn't been kidnapped and he wasn't mentally incompetent. How could she explain to the cops why she feared for his safety?

She would have followed them herself and brought him back, but at the rate they'd roared onto the highway, they'd be too far ahead for her to catch up. And they could have taken any direction, headed for Chicago, Key West, New York or Los Angeles. Even if they didn't kill him for his money, she'd probably never see him again. A yawning emptiness opened within her at the thought.

Fighting back tears, she settled in a swing on the restaurant's playground, pushing sluggishly back and forth with the toe of her shoe. Images of Rand fast-forwarded through her mind—Rand catching his first glimpse of television; bringing flowers for her hair; brushing her forehead with his lips; sprawled asleep across the sofa bed; holding her close when Angelina reappeared.

She remembered the tenderness of his smile and the rugged beauty of his body, poised on the edge of the spa pool. And his uncanny ability to read her. He'd pegged her pretty accurately in the few hours he'd known her, recognizing her for the lonely, work-driven woman she'd refused to see herself.

Work. She'd forgotten entirely about the Money Man campaign. Somehow even the Benson, Jurgen and Ives account didn't seem quite so important anymore. She'd have to call Kristin to cancel her previous instructions.

And then what? Back to the Bellevue? The hotel with its elegant ambience and romantic setting held no appeal without Rand to share it with her. She'd go back for the clothes she'd left behind, then return to Atlanta.

She pushed the swing faster. Just as well he had left. She'd become entirely too fond of him. If they'd spent many more days together, her determination to remain free of emotional involvement would have been seriously jeopardized. Dragging her toe, she stopped the swing and walked toward her car, head down, aching from the void his absence carved in her heart.

"Ready to go?"

Her head snapped up in surprise at the sound of his voice, and she spotted him leaning against the passenger door of her Toyota. Part of her longed to run to him and wrap her arms around him, while another part wanted nothing more than to smack his face for the worry he'd caused.

His eyes glowed like a child's at Christmas. "Those machines are magnificent. If I were going to remain in your time, I'd buy the biggest one I could find and explore the country on it."

"I thought you were gone." Her voice cracked on the last word.

He circled the car, placed his hands on her shoulders and turned her gently to face him. "You were really worried, weren't you?"

She nodded, not trusting her voice.

"But I was only gone a few minutes. I'd have been back sooner if I'd had better luck catching a ride."

She gazed up at him, puzzled. "They let you go?"

"They were doing me a favor." He slid his hands down her arms and laced his fingers with hers. "I was admiring their machines while you telephoned, and

Jericho, the big man we noticed inside, asked if I'd like a ride. He offered to take me a few miles down the road."

"Didn't you know I'd be frantic?" Now that he was safe, anger took relief's place.

"Those motorcycles are incredible, every bit as thrilling as horses." His smoke-colored eyes radiated excitement. "We covered a little over a mile before he dropped me off, but it's not a well-traveled road. I had to wait awhile before someone picked me up to bring me back."

Her anger now equaled her former despair and she snarled at him through clenched teeth. "Don't ever, ever do that to me again."

He released her hands. "What is it? Afraid of losing your precious Money Man?"

The bitterness in his voice stung her, and she looked away from the stern set of his jaw, the tightened mouth and eyes that glittered like case-hardened steel; but her anger was too fresh and raw to fade completely.

"We've got a deal, remember?" she flung at him.

He jerked open the car door for her. "Then we'd better get moving so you can keep your part of it."

She slipped into the driver's seat, expecting him to slam the door behind her, but he simply pushed it shut, then circled the car and climbed in. He pulled his sunglasses from his pocket and put them on.

As she drove onto the interstate, she was grateful that the mirrored surface of his lenses spared her further viewing of the anger and disappointment in his eyes.

Why had she panicked so at his disappearance? Two days ago she hadn't known Randolph Trent existed. What difference would it make if he left her life as quickly and unexpectedly as he'd entered it?

She ignored the inner voice telling her she'd have a hole in her heart big enough to drive a Mack truck through if Rand disappeared. Instead she concentrated on her Money Man campaign. She'd call Kristin at their next stop to check on her assistant's progress with the details.

By THE TIME they reached Valdosta they'd left the Florida heat behind. Low, angry clouds scudded across a dull, gunmetal sky, hiding a pale disc of sun. A stiff north wind bit through her jacket and lightweight slacks as she filled the tank with gas at an exit convenience store. As she replaced the gas cap, Rand waved to her from inside, indicating he'd settle up what she owed.

Clearing the pumps, she drove to the corner of the building and a pay phone. Her receptionist put her through to Kristin within seconds.

"Tory, you lucky dog. We're freezing our tushes off up here. How 'bout sending some of that hot Florida sunshine our way?"

Tory wiped sleeting rain from her face. No need yet for Kristin to know about her wild-goose chase to North Carolina. "How are the Money Man preparations coming?"

"Josh is working on ad copy and Susan's started the script. Stan has the art department making preliminary sketches. We'll have a full presentation ready when you're back from vacation." Her assistant's pleasant voice bubbled over the line.

"You're a wonder, Kristin. Remind me to talk to you about a raise when I return." She smiled, picturing the tiny woman with dark hair, eyes like a summer sky and enough energy to power the state of Georgia.

"Tory?" Kristin's voice turned solemn. "Forget this campaign for now and enjoy yourself. This is your first vacation in ages. I have everything under control."

She appreciated Kristin's concern, but she'd never been able to abandon a project once she'd started it. "Leave me a message at the hotel if you have any problems."

She found Rand still at the counter in the store. While a clerk took her order for a large black coffee, another filled a sack with Rand's purchases—corn chips, potato chips, Ding-Dongs, Ho-Hos, Twinkies, cheese crackers and Snickers bars. He sipped a giant cola as they returned to the car.

"Expecting a famine?" She started the engine.

"Just a little something to tide me over until dinner. Want some?" The steel in his jaw softened as he offered her the bag. Evidently he'd chosen to forgive her earlier outburst of temper.

She shook her head. "Have to watch my weight, remember?"

He unwrapped a Snickers bar, took a bite and chewed thoughtfully. "These are delicious. I can't get used to all this food, prepackaged and ready to eat. Someone must have made a fortune off these ideas.''

Money again. His focus was predictable, so why did she feel disappointed? ''We call it junk food.''

''Junk?''

''As in garbage.''

His contented chewing slowed. He swallowed. ''Why?''

''Because they have tons of calories and little nutritive value. You're better off eating fresh fruits and vegetables.'' She squirmed in her seat, realizing she sounded like her mother.

''But would I be enjoying it as much?''

His seductive baritone sent a tremor of pleasure through her, more satisfying than a sugar high, strumming every nerve ending in her body. She struggled to remain objective, reminding herself that his voice alone guaranteed success for her business.

''Are you saying you're a hedonist?'' she teased.

At first he didn't answer, and as she drove northward into the deepening twilight to the swishing rhythm of wiper blades and the plaintive notes of Dolly Parton, she feared she'd offended him.

When the song ended, Rand leaned forward and turned off the radio. ''Until I came here, the only pleasure in my life was my work. I slept because I needed to, ate because it was set before me, and I had no time for diversions. But whatever happened to me night before last sharpened my senses. I'm inundated with sights and sounds, tastes and smells like never before.''

The heated air of the enclosed car intensified the pleasingly masculine scent of him. "Don't you think that's true of anyone in a new environment?"

He shook his head and held his hands out before him, considering them as if he'd never seen them before. "My fingers tingle in response to textures I've never noticed. It's as if before my body was dead to the world around it, and now it's suddenly come alive."

He lay back against the headrest and from the corner of her eye she watched him taking in the passing scenery. He'd adjusted to a new century with remarkable confidence. He must have been truly formidable in his own time and place.

Rand closed his eyes, remembering the velvet smoothness of her skin and the delicate gossamer of her hair beneath his fingers. Her magnolia fragrance tortured him with a longing that flared in his groin. For a moment at the restaurant, he'd imagined affection mixed with the worry in her eyes, but he should have known she worried only for the profit his part in her campaign would bring her. In the end, money was all that had mattered to Selena. Why should he expect women of the 1990s to be any different?

TORY TURNED into the driveway and eased into the garage of her antebellum-style house in the Atlanta suburb. After removing the suitcases from the trunk, Rand followed her along the cloistered walkway into the kitchen.

"Just leave the bags there for now." She pointed to the mudroom. "We'll carry them up after dinner."

He dropped the suitcases and trailed behind her into the airy kitchen with its high ceiling, white cabinets and granite-topped island. She plucked up a note propped prominently against a verdant trailing ivy on the counter and read the barely legible scrawl.

"Nellie says she's left lasagna and salad in the fridge."

He looked up from the food processor he'd been inspecting. "Fridge?"

She opened the refrigerator door with a flourish and withdrew a covered casserole and Tupperware container filled with salad. Then she stopped short before picking up a bottle off the counter by the refrigerator. "Good grief, who'd have believed this?"

"It's a bottle of wine, one of the few items in here I recognize," he said.

She made a face at him. "I know it's wine. But Nellie would never buy this. She's a teetotaler."

"Maybe she fell off the wagon."

"Not that kind of teetotaler. She's never had a drink in her life. It's against her religion. That's why I'm shocked she bought this—but it will go great with the lasagna."

He studied the label of the Valpolicella. "Was 1991 a good year?"

"It was a great year."

She remembered the kitchen as it was when her family fixed Sunday supper together, with Jill setting the places at the island where they sat on tall stools to eat, her mother stirring her famous Portuguese stone soup on the stove top, and her father filling wineglasses while she tossed salad. She could almost hear their laughter and smell the spicy aroma of leeks and pepperoni. Until now, without her family, the room had seemed cold and sterile.

"How about some supper?" Rand's voice broke through her memories. "I'll open the wine."

"How can you be hungry?" He'd transformed his cache of junk food into a litter bag of wrappers during the course of their journey.

"I'm *always* hungry."

She turned hastily away from the heat in his eyes and rummaged in the drawer for the corkscrew. Then she popped the casserole in the microwave and frozen garlic bread in the oven. Within minutes, succulent aromas permeated the room and Rand, humming a Garth Brooks tune in a husky baritone as he filled the wineglasses, drove her loneliness away.

"Here." He handed her a glass. "How about a toast?"

As she took the glass from him, his fingers brushed hers, sending a delicious tingle up her arm. "To what?"

He raised his glass to hers. "To the success of tomorrow's mission."

"Tomorrow's mission." She clinked her glass against his, avoiding his eyes. Success for Rand meant finding a way to return to his time. Success for her meant keeping him with her—at least long enough for her ad campaign.

She sipped the full-bodied wine, then set her glass aside as she put out bright Mediterranean print place mats, flatware and dishes. A feeling of well-being penetrated her body and she realized with a jolt she felt truly happy for the first time since her parents' deaths. With Rand there with her, the big house embraced her with warmth, light, and treasured memories instead of mocking her with its emptiness. Once again it felt like home.

The microwave dinged and she withdrew the bubbling casserole and placed it on the island.

"Amazing. This was stone-cold minutes ago." He held his hand above its radiating heat, and his face held the stunned look of a man who'd witnessed miracles.

She filled glasses with ice and water from spigots in the refrigerator door. "You'll take all these conveniences for granted after you've lived here awhile."

"Here?"

"In this time." But that wasn't what she'd meant.

She drank more of her wine as her mind swirled with images of Rand in her house, eating in her kitchen, working in her garden, *sleeping in her bed*.

She set down her glass and examined it curiously. Maybe alcohol didn't agree with her. Lately, every time she drank, she either lost her concentration or her imagination ran wild.

Later, after Rand had polished off the last of Nellie's lasagna, then scraped plates into the disposal while she loaded the dishwasher, she carried a tray of coffee and mugs into the den and set them on the table before the sofa.

Portraits of her parents on their twenty-fifth wedding anniversary and silver-framed graduation pictures of Jill and her stared down at her from the mantel. Her family would have liked Randolph Trent.

He inspected the stone fireplace that covered one wall. "How about a fire? I assume you still build them the same way, unless you have some magic gadget that does it for you."

"A fire would be perfect, and we still build them the old-fashioned way, one log at a time."

She wondered if they'd had gas logs in his day as she curled her legs beneath her in the corner of the sofa, luxuriating in the comfort of the book-lined room with its overstuffed chairs and wall of French doors that overlooked the garden. She hadn't spent any time there since before her parents died. It had seemed so desolate without them. How could she have forgotten its reassuring, homey ambience?

Rand knelt by the elevated stone hearth, placing logs and kindling across the andirons. His jeans tightened across the hardness of his thighs and, as he reached to light the paper beneath the kindling, the muscles of his back and shoulders drew taut under his knitted pullover. When the kindling caught and fire licked the oak logs, he turned, flashing a megawatt smile that left her breathless.

He accepted the mug of coffee she handed him and settled into the opposite corner of the sofa. "This house—it's different."

Her breathing returned to normal, but a pleasurable warmth suffused her. "Other than electricity and modern appliances, it can't be that different from what you're used to. It was built in 1880."

The space between his dark brows creased thoughtfully as he surveyed the room, then turned his probing gaze to her. "It's not its age. More a question of atmosphere."

She ducked her head toward her mug, blocking out the leaping flames reflected in his eyes but unable to smother the corresponding heat spreading deep inside her. She gulped the hot coffee, which seemed tepid compared to the glow spreading outward from her body's core to her fingertips. If the atmosphere heated up any more, her whole body would go into meltdown.

She refilled her mug, hoping the caffeine would counteract whatever the wine had done to her senses. "Tell me about your home in Chicago."

The light died in his eyes. "It's more like a museum than a home. High ceilings, cold marble floors, Regency furniture."

She pictured an orphaned little boy wandering the lonely corridors. "Surely as a child you had a nursery, a playroom?"

"My uncle didn't believe in play."

"Then what did you do for fun?"

"My uncle didn't believe in fun, either."

"What *did* your uncle believe in?" She regretted that his uncle was long dead, because she'd have loved to give the old miser a piece of her mind for depriving Rand of childhood pleasures.

"Uncle Cyrus believed in hard work—and the money that resulted from it. He taught me himself, filling my days with mathematics and languages. For entertainment we studied the financial pages. He'd give me small sums to invest and every week we'd chart my progress."

Poor little kid. "But what about Christmas? Didn't you believe in Santa Claus? Didn't your uncle give you toys?"

He shook his head. "He gave the servants Christmas Day off, so we'd have a cold supper on our own." Sadness etched his face. "But he always gave me a larger sum for investing as a Christmas present."

His uncle sounded like a character straight from the pen of Charles Dickens. No wonder Rand thought of nothing but money. "Didn't you miss toys and the kinds of games other children played?"

He shrugged, acting as if it hadn't mattered. "You don't miss what you've never had."

But when she looked into the deep gray of his eyes, she read the wistfulness there. As she recalled Christmases spent in that room—the tall Scotch pine decorated with golden ornaments and red velvet bows, flickering bayberry candles, presents and laughter, hugs and kisses, and the aroma of turkey and sweet-potato pie wafting in from the kitchen—she longed to share those experiences with the man across from her.

Somewhere in the deep recesses of her mind, thoughts clamored to be released, fleeting recollections of her dependent mother and her Money Man campaign, but she couldn't capture them through the comfortable buzz the wine had created in her head. Relaxing in the romantic glow of the fire and Rand's stimulating presence, she rose and turned on the sound system.

Rand followed her, circling his arms around her waist from behind as she twisted a dial on the machine. He buried his face in the softness of her hair, scented like a sultry summer night. "You're a remarkable woman, Victoria Caswell."

Strains of music flooded the room. She turned in his arms and lifted her face to his with a shake of her head. "Just your typical female of the nineties."

He pulled her closer, swaying to the music. "Even in these extraordinary times, I'm certain you're different from other women."

She laid her head against his shoulder, muffling her voice against his sweater. "What a lovely thing to say."

As her body pressed the length of his, desire rolled through him like a tidal surge, accompanied by an overwhelming tenderness. He tightened one hand against the small of her back and smoothed her silky hair with the other.

Suddenly she pulled away and gazed at him, mischief glittering in her eyes. "What do you think is so remarkable about me?"

He resisted the impulse to kiss the tip of her up-turned nose. "Fishing for compliments?"

"You started this, remember?"

He tucked her head against his shoulder and moved to the music once more. "I'll give you a list of your attributes. Will that satisfy you?"

"Yes," she mumbled, nestling closer.

A distant part of his mind rattled at his consciousness, berating his inappropriate behavior and neglect of business, needling him with memories of Selena, but a cheerful buzzing in his brain, probably caused by the wine, soon drowned out the unwanted thoughts. He turned his attention completely to the woman in his arms.

"Where were we?" he asked.

"The list."

The music soared and he twirled her around the room, holding her closer with each turn. "Compassion would be at the top."

"Compassion?" She stopped and gazed at him with puzzlement.

"Who else would have taken in a perfect stranger so readily and with such kindness? I bet you're a sucker for stray animals."

"You call it compassion." Her eyes filled with laughter. "I call it insanity."

"Whatever it is—" he brushed his lips across her forehead " —it's irresistible."

He caught the flush that colored her cheeks before she hid her face against his chest once more.

"Is that all?" her muffled voice teased him.

The sharp intake of his breath whistled between his teeth. "Would you like me to kiss you again?"

"I'll take the fifth on that question. I was referring to the list. You can't have a real list with only one word." She moved her hands along his shoulders until cool fingers stroked the back of his neck.

He struggled to concentrate on her words. "A glutton for praise, eh?"

"One can never receive too much praise. It's like being too rich or too thin."

He spanned her midriff with his hands. "You're not too thin."

She glanced at him with eyes that reminded him of sunlight dancing on water, then playfully swatted his shoulder. "In this day and age that is *not* a compliment."

Her rosy lips parted slightly with laughter, revealing small white teeth. Mesmerized, he lowered his lips, hesitantly at first. Then he crushed his mouth to hers at the welcome pressure of her response. With searching hands, he unclasped the gold barrette at her nape and buried his fingers in her flowing hair.

Tory twined her arms tighter around his neck, drawing him closer. Her knees weakened at the hot sweetness of his kiss, and she swayed dizzily against him, gripping his shoulders to keep from falling, losing herself in the pleasurable sensations his lips ignited.

The heat of his body scorched the length of her, and his heart hammered against her breasts. Passion and desire inflamed her senses, drowning her reason in a sea of yearning.

The loud, harsh ring of the telephone broke the spell.

He drew back, gazing at her with eyes of swirling smoke. His voice seemed to come at her from a distance as she broke the surface of desire.

"What's that?" His voice was hoarse with emotion.

Still trembling from the effects of his kiss, she pushed her hair off her face. "The telephone."

He released her, and for a second she feared her unstable legs would collapse. She teetered to the sofa and sank into its deep cushions, waiting for her swirling senses to steady.

"Shouldn't you answer it?"

She brushed the back of her hand across her swollen lips. "The answering machine will get it."

"Answering machine?"

At his look of disbelief, she pulled to her feet, took him by the hand and led him into the hallway. On the maple table against the stairwell, the recorder whirred to life.

"Sorry I can't take your call now. Please leave your name and number and I'll get back to you," her recorded voice announced.

"That's you." His eyebrows shot up in surprise.

The machine beeped and an aluminum siding salesman began his pitch. She quickly lifted the receiver and replaced it, and the obnoxious voice ceased.

Rand scratched his head as he watched her erase and rewind the tape. "Every time I think I'm becoming accustomed to modern living, I encounter a new invention. How much else is there?''

''You've only scratched the surface.''

His gaze burned into her. ''I look forward to exploring more deeply.''

She started as the grandfather clock in the hallway struck eleven o'clock and turned away from his uncomfortable scrutiny. ''We have to make an early start in the morning if we're to meet with Smallwood at eleven. If you'll bring up the bags, I'll show you to your room.''

Every nerve in her body quivered with his nearness as she mounted the stairs before him. At the top, she paused. ''Set my bag here, please. Your room's in the other direction.''

Without speaking, he deposited her luggage, then followed her to the far end of the hall, where she threw open the door of the guest room.

''You should be comfortable here. I asked Nellie to put fresh linens on the bed and in the adjoining bath.''

She pointed to the bathroom door, avoiding his eyes. If only she could make it to her room and close the door before she made a total fool of herself and fell into his arms again.

He placed his bag atop the blanket chest at the foot of the bed, then turned to her. ''About earlier—''

''If there's anything else you need, my room's at the other end of the hall.'' She smiled weakly, hoping her words hadn't sounded like an invitation, then hurried out of the room before he could respond.

She picked up her bag at the head of the stairs and lugged it into her room, throwing it onto the bed.

What was the matter with her? She'd behaved like a lovesick puppy, or worse, a love-starved woman.

Well? an inner voice taunted.

"Shut up," she growled and went into the bathroom to throw cold water on her overheated face.

Then she removed her clothes, dressed in a brushed flannel gown, set her alarm for five o'clock and crawled between the smooth sheets of her poster bed. She'd driven over four hundred miles and her body ached with fatigue. When her head hit the pillow, she drifted off into sleep.

SHE AWOKE SUDDENLY, shivering with cold. The red digits of her alarm winked two o'clock, but she couldn't get back to sleep with the cold draft permeating the room. Nellie must have left a window open. She rolled to the other side of the bed, threw back the covers and sat up. Her body froze at the sight before her.

Glowing in the early morning darkness, the ghost of Angelina Fairchild stood at her door.

Chapter Seven

Victoria's scream jerked Rand from a dreamless sleep. He bolted blindly down the unlighted hallway to her room and flung open the door. Pausing on the threshold, he peered into the unbroken darkness.

"Victoria?"

Pale light flooded the room as she switched on a lamp by her bed and sat huddled against the headboard, hugging her knees to her chest beneath a flowing azure gown that matched her startled eyes.

Emotions washed over him, stronger than he'd believed possible. Foremost arose the desire to protect her, to insure that harm never touched one golden hair of her head.

"What's wrong?" His voice, thick with sleep, sounded strange in his ears.

"Angelina was here."

The sharp chill of the room bit into his bare chest, and he couldn't tell if she shivered from cold or fright. "Are you certain? Maybe it was only a dream."

She shook her head. "I was awake, and she disappeared when I screamed."

In two long strides he crossed the room and gathered her into his arms, pulling her tightly against him to ease her shaking. Smoothing her tawny hair, he rocked her gently, like a child. "She can't harm you. She's only a spirit."

"I know. But she scared the living daylights out of me. I never expected to see her here, not in my own room." She nestled closer in his embrace, and the contact of her cheek against his bare chest sent his blood thundering through his veins.

Most women he'd known would have fainted dead away at the appearance of such a terrifying specter, but not Victoria. His admiration for her courage grew as his senses surrendered to her seductive perfume, the brightness in her eyes and the soft curves of her body pressing against him. Fighting to control the tide of passion surging through him, he lifted a finger and traced the line of her cheek.

"We have a long journey tomorrow. You need your rest." Tenderness weighted his voice.

She stirred and stretched, glancing at the clock. "I could really use a few hours more sleep, but I can't close my eyes now. Every time I do, I see the terrible despair on her face."

He noted the heaviness of her eyelids and the weariness of her movements. "You're the one who's driving tomorrow. Go back to sleep while I keep watch."

He stood, intending to pass the rest of the night in the chair by her bed, but she grasped his hand. "No need for both of us to lose sleep. Stay here with me."

"Are you sure?" He searched her face for a sign of desire that matched his own and discovered only fatigue and a lingering trace of fright.

Immediately she curled on her side away from him and closed her eyes, squelching any of his lingering amorous hopes. He lifted the covers and slid in beside her, sculpting his body to hers. He slipped one arm around her narrow waist, drawing her close, hoping in her drowsy state she wouldn't notice the hard evidence of the effect she had on him.

Slumbering, she placed her hand over his and continued the deep, steady breathing of sleep. He held her, marveling at the pleasure she brought him, contemplating her presence in his bed each night and resigning himself to storing memories of her, molded against his body like a spoon within a spoon.

His heart and head argued, the first tempting him with the possibility of spending the rest of his nights with Victoria in his arms, the latter reminding him of the importance of his meeting with Jason Phiswick and the perfidy of women.

His internal argument and Victoria's tantalizing presence banished all possibility of sleep. A few minutes before five, he quietly left her bed and returned to his room to dress.

TORY EXITED the Atlanta bypass and entered the stream of traffic on Interstate 85 that would carry them east toward Charlotte and Raleigh. The rising sun glimmered just below the horizon of a rosy sky washed clean by yesterday's rain.

Since awakening that morning she'd avoided mentioning the past night. As she recalled Rand's kiss, a glow crept up her cheeks, and she pledged to give up alcohol. It made her do and think too many crazy things.

But most of all, she remembered his bursting into her room after Angelina's unexpected visit, standing beside her bed wearing only the pants of his pajamas. His thick, tangled hair had tumbled over his broad forehead, and his eyes, heavy with sleep, had glowed silver in the lamplight. The instant his arms had encircled her, her distress had vanished and she'd fallen asleep feeling secure, protected.

Past that point her recollections wavered. He hadn't been there when she awoke. Had he really climbed into her bed and held her against him while she slept? Had she dreamed the pressure of his hard arousal searing through her flannel gown?

She thrust aside the memories and glanced at him, dozing in the seat beside her. Returning her attention to the morning traffic, she recalled the ghost of Angelina. Her scream at Angelina's appearance had been one of surprise, not fear. She'd felt no threat from the unhappy young woman.

Rand stirred and stretched. "Where are we?"

"Almost to Greenville. There's an exit soon. Are you ready for some coffee?"

"Sounds good. And a bite to eat."

She repressed a smile. His idea of a snack would feed a family of four. "I'm glad you could catch up on your sleep. Sorry I awakened you in the middle of the night."

"I'm not," he stated bluntly. He fiddled with the radio until he captured the signal of a country music station. The sounds of dueling banjos filled the car. "Why do you think Angelina's ghost followed you to Atlanta?"

She shrugged. "The first time I encountered her, she was searching for her lost love. Maybe she believes I can help her find him."

"But by now he's as dead as she is."

"Angelina doesn't know that. I've read about spirits who haunt places because of some unresolved emotional turmoil right before their deaths."

"What places?"

"The South is full of them—houses, railroad crossings, bridges, even mountains. When I was a little girl, I once read an entire book just on North Carolina's ghosts."

He settled back against the seat. "Uncle Cyrus would have never approved such reading matter. He wouldn't have thought it—"

"Practical?" She smiled when he nodded. "I feel I'm getting to know your uncle well."

"He wouldn't have approved of you, either, and you can take that as the compliment it's intended." He lowered the volume on the banjos. "Now, what were you saying about Angelina?"

"Emma told me Angelina had quarreled with her lover and when she died, she lost forever the chance for reconciliation." The absurdity of her situation mocked her, talking about ghosts with a man from another century. She might be stone-cold sober, but that didn't mean she wasn't crazy.

"So if you can convince Angelina her lover is also dead, you believe she might cease and desist from her haunting?" he asked.

"It's worth a try. She's popped into my life every night since Jill's wedding. It's a habit I'd like to break."

"If she holds true to her pattern, you'll have that chance tonight."

Tonight. By that evening they'd have seen Smallwood, and Rand would have learned that his quest was futile. Then he'd have to uphold his part of the bargain and prepare for the Money Man campaign. Just as well. Being busy would keep his mind off his disappointment.

A scratching sound drew her attention to her passenger, who scribbled rapidly in a small notebook.

"What's that?" she asked.

"Just some notes and calculations for my meeting with Jason Phiswick this weekend. I plan to earn us both a great deal of money." He continued to write, covering page after page, stopping now and then to gaze at the ballpoint pen with amazement as he clicked the button that operated the nib.

"Isn't there anything—anyone in your life except business?" she asked.

His writing slowed, then stopped. "There was once. It was a mistake."

"It?"

"She."

"Does *she* have a name?"

"Selena. But I'd rather not talk about her." He stared at the highway for a long minute, then resumed his scribbling.

Did he find talking about Selena painful because he still loved her? Was it this Selena, not his love of making money, pulling him back to his own time?

A Carolina freight truck roared past, buffeting her car in its vortex. She glanced at her speedometer; she was driving well below the limit.

Delaying your arrival? her conscience taunted her. *Afraid Smallwood might have the answer to sending Rand back?*

She pressed the accelerator, pushing the car up to speed, stifling her inner voice with a silent declaration of a strictly business interest in Randolph Trent. When they stopped for coffee in Greenville, she'd call Kristin and arrange an immediate meeting for Rand with her staff.

He flipped shut his notebook and tucked it into the pocket of his sports jacket. "Turnabout is fair play."

She abandoned her mental cataloging of instructions for Kristin. "What do you mean?"

"Is there anything in *your* life except business?"

The heat of his gaze targeted her like a laser. "I date—occasionally."

"But what about marriage? Family?"

She searched for hints of derision in his tone but found only curiosity. "Things have changed in the past hundred years. Not all women want to marry."

"But without husbands, who takes care of them?"

She grinned at his assumption. "They take care of themselves. Women today have jobs outside the home. Many own their own businesses, like me, and others are professionals—accountants, lawyers, doctors—"

"Female doctors?" He sounded doubtful. "I've heard of a few, but no one takes them seriously."

From the corner of her eye, she caught his dubious expression. "They do now. Female doctors aren't unusual, not with over fifty percent of all women engaged somewhere in the work force."

"But if over half the women are working, who's having the babies?" He gazed out over the congested interstate. "There're too many people for the birth rate to have dropped in the last hundred years."

"With modern methods of birth control, women can plan their pregnancies." She blushed, remembering his Victorian sensibilities. "They're still having children, but in their own time, not by accident."

"And their husbands agree to this?"

"If they have a husband."

His expression turned incredulous. "Children are still conceived . . . the same way?"

Mischief tugged at the corners of her mouth, and she struggled to keep a straight face. "For the most part."

He leaned toward her, searching her face as if doubting her truthfulness. "There's another way?"

"Women who want children without a husband opt for artificial insemination with donated sperm." She tried to imagine the impact of such knowledge on his Victorian mind and failed.

"Children without fathers? Would *you* consider such a thing?"

She shook her head. "I believe children need a mother and a father."

He lay back against the headrest as if the conversation had exhausted him. "It's reassuring to know the family hasn't gone completely out of style."

She smiled, remembering. "My parents were two of the happiest people I knew. Jill and I are lucky to have had such a warm and loving family."

"Then surely you plan to marry and have children someday?"

She thought of her mother. "No. I'll never marry."

"Then you'll be—"

"An old maid?" She spoke the words before he could. "But I'll be a wealthy, successful old maid with a thriving company to keep me busy."

"But will it keep you happy?"

His question probed too deep, angering her. "You're a fine one to talk."

He shifted in his seat, stretching long legs before him, reviving memories of his body pressed against hers in the night. "It's different with me."

"Why?"

"I'm a man."

"Of all the chauvinistic, old-fashioned—" She bit off the earthy expletive that sizzled on her tongue, one she doubted even men used in his day, and searched her vocabulary for an appropriate Victorian response. "Balderdash."

"But marriage and children are an integral part of woman's nature," he insisted.

"Men in this century have acknowledged the importance of love and family, too." She flung the words at him, seeing too late the trap she'd set for herself.

"Then we're a pair, aren't we, Victoria Caswell?" His voice caressed her with understanding.

She lowered her window slightly, and the frigid air cooled her flushed face. But emotions continued to tumble within her, uncomfortable feelings, dangerous feelings that threatened the secure monotony of her life.

He pointed to a sign as they whizzed by. "You missed the Greenville exit."

"We don't have time to stop."

The sooner they reached Raleigh, the sooner they could return and begin work on the Money Man project. And the sooner she could rid her life of Rand Trent, who threatened her tranquillity with questions of love and children and memories of his body melded with hers.

TORY'S DECISION to press forward proved wise because the trip took longer than she'd counted on. As she exited the interstate onto Hillsborough Avenue in Raleigh, the dashboard clock registered ten-thirty. She continued down the traffic-thronged street, past Meredith College on a hilltop to their left, past shops and stores, and headed into downtown, toward the Capitol.

The smokestacks and massive brick buildings of North Carolina State University rose on the right, spread out upon a campus of dead grass and leafless trees, a dreary sight even under the brilliant blue of the February sky. She turned onto the campus at a street beside the bell tower and pulled into visitor parking near the administration building.

"I have to make a call." She pointed to a pay phone against a nearby building.

Rand exited the car and stretched. "I'll find out where to locate Dr. Smallwood."

As she placed her call to Kristin, she watched him take the steps to the administration building two at a time. A cluster of passing coeds stopped to admire his lean body and dark good looks, and their giggling words floated toward her on the crisp winter breeze.

"Nice buns," observed a tall slender girl in jeans and a down-filled vest.

"He's so fine, he could park his shoes under my bed any time," suggested another.

A short dumpling of a woman in a brief skirt and tights tossed long hair over her shoulders as she watched

Rand disappear through the double doors. "I wouldn't mind making a love connection with him myself."

Her tall friend jabbed her in the ribs with an elbow. "In your dreams."

The plump girl flipped her hair again. "On second thought, maybe he's too old for me. He must be at least thirty."

The laughing girls passed Tory as she finished her call. She could understand their reaction. His extraordinary good looks invited instant attention, but the man's attraction was more than skin-deep. An aura of confidence and integrity surrounded him, proclaiming him a man you could trust. The perfect Money Man for her campaign.

The perfect man to love. She jammed her fists into her jacket pockets. She refused to surrender her independence, even for the perfect man.

In minutes he joined her. With the sun glinting off his hair, his eyes reflecting the pearl gray of his turtleneck sweater, the muscled contours of his body filling out his blue jacket and dark slacks and his handsome jaw jutting aggressively into the wind, he made passing college men appear awkward and immature by comparison.

"Smallwood's office is in Cox Hall. It's just a short hike across campus," he said.

"Good thing I wore comfortable shoes."

The excitement on his face worried her. How was he going to feel when Smallwood dashed all hope of returning to his own time? She longed to drag her feet to delay the moment, but he grasped her arm and led her off at a quick walk between towering dormitories and classroom buildings toward the campus center.

When they entered a large quadrangle, he halted and took his bearings. "There's the library and opposite it the round building they told me to look for. Cox Hall, the physics building, is just past there."

Pulling her along, he skirted the cylindrical structure, striding toward Cox Hall in long, purposeful steps.

She stopped, winded, and grabbed at the stitch in her side. "Out of shape," she huffed. "I haven't jogged since before Jill's wedding."

"Sorry. I wasn't thinking—" His face fell with remorse.

She held up a hand to staunch his protests. "It's okay. I've caught my breath now."

When he started forward again, he moved at a more accommodating pace and she had no trouble keeping up with him, even as they climbed the steep stairs to the second floor of the physics building. The hallways, smelling of steam heat, chalk dust and musty books, flooded suddenly with youthful bodies as the class hour changed. Rand flattened himself against a wall and drew her alongside him as a nearby doorway erupted with students.

When the tide of humanity ebbed, he took her hand as they followed the corridor to its last doorway. Her fingers clasped the warmth of his flesh, and she regretted the loss of contact when he dropped her hand to knock.

No one answered. She glanced at her watch. "It's eleven on the nose. Maybe his morning class ran late."

"Maybe he's the typical absentminded professor and forgot we had an appointment." He balled his fist and knocked again.

From behind the door came a muffled exclamation and the sound of books hitting the floor. Then the door swung open and a fresh-faced young man with short-cropped, sandy hair and wire-rimmed glasses peered out at them. "Yes?"

She thrust her hand forward. "Victoria Caswell. We spoke on the phone yesterday, Dr. Smallwood."

Smallwood's befuddled expression cleared as he shook her hand. "Of course, our appointment. I'd completely forgotten."

Rand shot her an I-told-you-so look before offering the man his hand. "Randolph Trent."

Smallwood stepped back from the door for them to enter. She squeezed first into the cubicle, smaller than her walk-in closet at home. Two large windows on the opposite wall threw feeble light into the narrow space, lined with bookshelves that overflowed into piles of books on the floor. She stepped around them toward a chair by Smallwood's desk.

Smallwood reached it before her, swiping a yard-high heap of student notebooks from the seat and stacking them precariously on the windowsill. From beneath another pile of what looked like debris, but obviously had some value from the careful way he transferred it, Smallwood extracted another chair for Rand.

The professor settled himself into his creaking desk chair across from them, leaned back and laced his fingers across his chest. "Now, what can I do for you?"

His wide blue eyes and smooth skin gave him the appearance of a kid playing grown-up. Was this the man Rand expected to help him leap a gap of one hundred years?

"My firm," she began, "has agreed to underwrite the production of Mr. Trent's screenplay."

Smallwood's sandy eyebrows peaked. "What kind of screenplay?"

"An adventure," Rand said.

"Does this adventure have a name?"

She glimpsed a flash of panic in Rand's eyes. *"The Man from Yesterday,"* she improvised. "It's about a time traveler."

Smallwood leaned forward, his blue eyes shining behind the thick lenses of his glasses. "Where do I fit in?"

"We need some technical advice," she said. "I've asked Mr. Trent to rewrite the ending, make it more plausible."

"Time travel plausible? You're putting me on."

"I read your article in the *Smithsonian* about the potential of moving through time and space," Rand said, "and knew you were the one to solve our dilemma."

Smallwood scratched the bridge of his nose thoughtfully. "Exactly what is your dilemma?"

"Today's audiences are sophisticated," Rand explained. "They no longer accept such concepts as being conveyed through time by a simple blow to the head. We have to present them with a situation that—''

''Allows them to suspend their disbelief,'' she said. ''Otherwise the film may bomb, and my firm loses its investment.''

She felt like a character in a movie herself, playing a part to keep her end of the bargain with Rand. She dreaded the moment when Smallwood ruined all his hopes.

Smallwood leaned back once more with interest quickening in his eyes. ''Tell me the story so far. I'll see what I can do.''

Rand cleared his throat. ''A man awakens in a hotel room to discover he's been projected one hundred years into the future. He has various adventures as he encounters the marvels of his new surroundings, but his main purpose always is to return to his own time.''

''There's a beautiful woman pining for him there, right?'' Smallwood grinned.

Her glance flashed to Rand. She noted his expression of discomfort and wondered at its significance.

''Er, right,'' Rand said. ''Now our problem is *how* to get him back where he belongs.''

She leaned forward, expecting Smallwood to deliver the coup de grace to Rand's hopes. ''In the context of our story, can the man really expect to return to his own time?''

Smallwood grew very still and his gaze bored into her. ''We're speaking theoretically, right?''

"Of course." She squirmed under the scrutiny of Smallwood's bright eyes, wise beyond their years.

He tapped the tips of his fingers together, forming a pyramid with his hands. "Then the answer is yes."

"Yes?" Smallwood's words struck like a boxer's punch in her solar plexus. As she struggled to breathe, hope illuminated Rand's face.

"Could you explain how this time travel would be accomplished?" he asked.

"Ever since Einstein's theory of relativity was interpreted by Minkowski," Smallwood began, "the science of physics has clearly dealt, not with two separate entities of time and space, but a singular entity—space-time."

The professor launched into a complex description of temporal cross sections, hypersurfaces, time lines bending back on themselves, black holes and quantum-mechanical aspects of time. Her head ached as she tried to follow.

Rand interrupted Smallwood's explanation of the findings of British cosmologist E. A. Milne. "Our audiences are sophisticated, but our story is intended only as entertainment. We don't want to overwhelm them with anything too technical. Could you illustrate in layman's terms how to send our character back?"

Smallwood nodded, grabbed a piece of paper from the chaos on his desk and began to sketch curving arcs. "Timelike world lines can bend back on themselves. At the point where a line touches itself, a person could pass through the temporal cross section."

Rand's eyes narrowed. "To the exact time and place he left?"

"If he enters the cross section in the same place and time as he left it—it's theoretically possible."

Rand nodded. "But our protagonist will spend several days in the future. Can he still return to the exact time he left?"

Smallwood wrinkled his forehead. "Since our entire discussion is theoretical, I can't assure you of that, but I believe he'd reenter his own time at least within a matter of days."

Tory's head spun with scientific terms. "I'm not sure I understand."

A look of infinite patience crossed Smallwood's face. "Let's take the character in your screenplay as an example. He awakens in a hotel room and finds he's traveled forward in time. If he wants to return, he must wait for the time line to bend back upon itself in that same room in order to go back to the space-time that he left."

"How soon would that temporal cross section open up again?" Rand asked.

"If at all," Smallwood said, "probably within a matter of days, at most a week or two. After that, the temporal cross section might reflect a different slice of space-time."

"Or it might not recur at all?" she asked.

"But for the purpose of your screenplay," Smallwood insisted with a grin, "it must."

Rand rose to his feet. "Thank you, Dr. Smallwood. You've given us the solution to our dilemma. We won't take any more of your time."

Smallwood ran a hand over his short hair, looking more boyish than ever. "You'll let me know when the movie's released?"

"You'll be the first one we notify," Tory called over her shoulder as Rand propelled her out the door.

She trotted to keep up with his long strides as he hurried from the building. Crossing the campus, he never slackened his pace. In frustration, she stopped short, grabbing his sleeve to act as a brake.

"Slow down," she gasped. "We're not running a marathon." She collapsed on a nearby bench.

"Catch your breath, then we must return to the hotel as quickly as possible." His voice vibrated with excitement as he sat beside her.

"What's the rush?"

"You heard what he said. The temporal cross section is most likely to occur within the next two weeks. If I miss it, I'll remain here forever."

She wanted to shake him. "*If* is the operative word here. *If* there is such a thing, if it will occur again. Don't you see that you're grasping at straws?"

Her heart ached for him and the life he'd lost, but the sooner he accepted he was stuck here, the better off he'd be.

He placed his hands on her shoulders and turned her to face him. "I have to take the chance. I've been ripped away from everything that's familiar to me. Backward and primitive as my time might seem to you, it's where I'm comfortable, where I belong.''

Desperation etched his face. She realized he'd never be satisfied until he'd exhausted every effort to return.

"If we return to the Bellevue for two weeks," he said, "and nothing happens, then I promise I'll fill my part of our bargain."

"But—"

"Besides," he added with an engaging grin, "you haven't finished your vacation."

She groaned inwardly. His insistence on returning to Florida not only delayed the Money Man campaign but it also placed her in close quarters with the man's undeniable charms for almost two more weeks.

But what choice did she have? She'd made a bargain and she'd stick to it, even though their return to the hotel would be a colossal waste of time, not to mention a terrible disappointment when he found himself still stuck in the 1990s in two weeks.

"Okay, you win." She rose and started down the walk toward the administration parking lot. "But we'll have to stop in Atlanta overnight. I'll be too tired to drive straight through."

Not to mention the meeting with her staff, but she'd tell him about that later.

Walking beside her, he frowned, looking ready to disagree. Then he threw his hands wide in a gesture of acceptance. "Back to Atlanta, then. But could we stop somewhere first for lunch? I could eat a horse."

RAND STUDIED Victoria's profile, illuminated by the headlights of eastbound traffic. He'd never met a woman like her. Beneath her soft, appealing exterior lay a determined and independent core. Like Selena, she knew what she wanted in life. Unlike Selena, Victoria wouldn't hurt others to get it.

Regret stabbed him as he considered saying farewell to the woman who'd given so freely of her time to assist him. Had he arrived in someone else's hotel room, he would probably have been jailed for breaking and entering or locked away in an asylum as a madman.

But not by Victoria. Good-hearted and generous, she'd volunteered to assist him from the start. No, she was nothing like Selena.

"Rand?" Her voice pulled him from his thoughts. "There's something I need to tell you before we reach the house."

The hesitancy in her tone alarmed him. "You haven't changed your mind about returning me to Florida?"

"No."

Her negative reply ended with an upward inflection, warning him of more to come, something he wasn't going to like. "Then what is it?"

Her hands tensed on the steering wheel. "There'll be some people waiting for us when we get to my house."

"People?" A sudden fear of exploitation gripped him. Had he been wrong about her? "Reporters?"

She glanced at him with horror. "Good grief, no. You must never speak to the press about your experience.

They'll serve you up to the public to enjoy at the breakfast table with their morning paper.''

He settled into his seat with a wry smile. "Not a pretty image for your Money Man, is it?"

"Not a pleasant experience for anyone to suffer."

The compassion in her voice made him regret his hasty condemnation of her motives. "Then who are these people I'm to meet at your home?"

She squirmed in her seat, keeping her eyes on the road ahead. "They're from my office. My executive assistant, the art director and a copywriter. I want to give them a head start on the Benson, Jurgen and Ives account."

He should have known her profitable campaign would be foremost in her mind. Then another thought struck him. He placed his hand on her arm, feeling the warmth of her through the sleeve of her jacket. "You don't believe I'm going back, do you?"

This time she gave no rising inflection to her word. Her flat, toneless *no* rang with finality and defeat.

"What if you're wrong?" he asked.

"I can live with it." She dropped one hand from the wheel and covered his hand on her arm. "But if you're wrong, can you?"

She squeezed his hand gently before replacing hers on the wheel, but his racing thoughts barely registered the contact. If he could close that stock agreement with Jason Phiswick, it would be the biggest deal he'd ever negotiated, setting him up with enough capital to build his fortune for the rest of his days. The challenge of it stirred his blood.

And if he didn't go back? He'd be lost forever in the future, homeless, practically penniless, forced to hawk the success of others in order to earn a meager living.

But Victoria would be there, a rebellious voice whispered in his mind. *And you'd have the challenge of building your fortune in a new world.*

"Could you live with never going back?" she repeated.

He closed his mind to the seductive inner voice. "I refuse to consider that possibility until I have no other choice."

WHEN VICTORIA'S staff had finally departed and Rand collapsed in a chair in her family room, he prayed fervently that Smallwood's theories would prove valid. Remembering the hours of posing for instant photographs from something called a Polaroid, of having his voice and moving image recorded on a video camera, of being poked and measured for costumes, he shuddered at the thought of earning his living in such a manner.

"I found some Scotch in Dad's study." Victoria entered the room with a bottle and a glass. "You look as if you could use a drink. I'm sorry my crew took so long. You must be exhausted."

"Join me?" He pulled himself upright to accept the offered glass.

She shook her head. "Alcohol doesn't agree with me lately."

He took a generous swallow, grateful for the heat that burned down his throat. "What now?"

She sat on the opposite end of the sofa and drew her knees to her chest. "To bed. We'll get an early start—"

A gust of wind blew open the French doors, banging them against the wall and filling the room with frigid air. He leapt to his feet to secure the doors. When he turned toward the sofa, the ghost of Angelina Fairchild stood in the center of the room between him and Victoria. Except for the unusual pallor of her complexion, the specter appeared as real and solid as he did.

"Help me," Angelina whimpered, "you must help me."

Victoria straightened where she sat and glanced toward him. He nodded encouragement. "Now's your chance."

"I want to help you, Angelina," she said in a soothing tone. "What is it you want?"

He admired the steadiness in Victoria's voice, the calmness of her demeanor. He eased into the armchair, hoping not to call attention to himself.

Angelina paced before the sofa, wringing her pale, slender hands. The folds of her turquoise dress swished, whispering as she walked, and strands of her dark hair lifted and flowed, although there was no breeze in the room. "Help me find him. I *must* find him."

"Who is he, this man you're seeking?" Victoria asked.

"The man I love," Angelina said, "Jason Phiswick."

"Phiswick!" The name exploded on his lips.

Angelina whirled at the sound and focused her attention on him. "You! You're his friend. You must know where he is."

He spread his hands and shrugged. "Jason died decades ago." He attempted to be gentle. "You're in the 1990s now, Angelina. You've been dead almost a hundred years."

"I can't be dead." The gaze of her watery blue eyes raked him. "You're not dead. Except for your strange clothes, you look exactly as you did when I last saw you, just a few days ago."

"He's right, Angelina." At the consoling sound of Victoria's voice, the specter turned to her. "You must let this life go. You drowned in a boating accident a long time ago—after your quarrel with Jason."

Angelina clasped her pale throat with a slender hand. "But I can't be dead." She lowered her hands, pressing them against her abdomen where the fabric of her dress pulled taut in fashionable tucks and pleats. "My baby— Jason's child—I have to tell him."

"Was that why you quarreled?" Rand asked.

Midnight black curls trembled as she shook her head. "He doesn't know. I'd planned a special picnic for Saturday on the island. I wanted a romantic setting when I gave him the happy news."

Puzzlement creased Victoria's forehead. "Then why did you quarrel?"

Angelina pointed a thin finger at him. "Because of you."

He registered the words with a sense of shock. "Me?"

Angelina's eyes blazed. "Jason rejected my plans for a picnic. He insisted he had an important meeting with you, a meeting that was crucial to his future—our future."

He sank into his chair. "But we haven't had that meeting yet." He glanced toward Victoria. "That's the meeting I must return for."

Angelina paced before the fireplace, creating eddies of freezing air as she passed. "He loved me. He was going to ask my father for permission for us to marry. Jason would have been pleased about the baby, I know he would."

"Angelina." Victoria rose from the sofa and approached the unhappy young woman. "It's too late. Don't you remember sailing for the island and the freak wind that overturned your boat?"

Angelina stopped her pacing and pressed her fists against her temples. "I don't want to remember."

"You must," Victoria insisted gently. "You drowned when the boat capsized. And even if Jason Phiswick were alive today, he'd be over one hundred and twenty years old. You must let this life go."

"No!"

Angelina's mournful cry made the hair on the back of Rand's neck stand on end. He watched Angelina approach Victoria with outstretched hands.

"You must help me find him. I'll make you help me!" Angelina reached for Victoria's throat.

Levering himself from his chair, he threw himself across the room between the two, knocking Victoria onto the sofa and falling across her protectively. If Angelina intended to attack Victoria, the ghost would have to go through him first.

Victoria stared at him with startled eyes and her breath warmed his cheek. Beneath him the soft curves of her body strained against his, and he raised himself on his elbows to prevent crushing her with his weight.

She glanced over his shoulder to survey the room. "Angelina's gone."

"Is she?" The threat of Angelina faded as his awareness of the woman beneath him increased.

"I don't think she would have hurt me, but thank you for—protecting me." Her breath stirred his hair.

"Victoria." He breathed her name like a prayer, then brushed his lips across her eyelids, the tip of her nose, down the delicate line of her jaw to the pulsing vein in the hollow of her throat. At her trembling response, he shifted his weight to one elbow, drawing her to him with his other arm. The heat of her body seared the length of him.

He shouldn't love this woman. It wasn't fair. Within two weeks he'd be gone from her life forever, never to return. He started to pull away, but her arms encircled his neck, drawing him closer, and passion silenced the voice of reason clamoring in his head.

She lifted her lips to his, and the sweet offering of her mouth blotted out all his thoughts, leaving only instincts to guide him. Consumed by a hunger that deepened to scorching demand, his mouth locked fiercely on hers. The power of her eager response jolted every cell in his body, sending his senses singing, heating his desire to fever pitch.

He outlined the lobe of her ear with his fingertips, then traced the curve of her shoulder, caressed the slender column of her neck, felt her blood pulsing there beneath his fingers. Slipping his hand into the neckline of her blouse, he stroked the silky smoothness of her skin.

Insistent fire spread through his loins—until he remembered Angelina. The young woman's plight, searching through the years for the father of her never-to-be-born child, sobered him. He drew back, breathing raggedly, and attempted to smile.

"There is no future in this. I cannot mislead you."

"Mislead?" Her eyes twinkled with mischief. "I thought you were kissing."

He half groaned, half laughed and pressed his fingers against her lips. "You must stop smiling at me like that or I won't be able to resist kissing you again."

Her smile widened. "Promise?"

He pushed away from her, intending to put as much distance between him and temptation as possible, but she held his arm. When he turned to her again, he observed the puzzled look that had replaced her smile.

"Did I do or say something wrong?" she asked.

He leaned toward her and brushed a sun gold curl from her forehead. "No. I'm the one who overstepped the mark."

"I don't understand." Her husky voice rekindled the desire he'd thought subdued.

"We mustn't—" He groped for the right words but couldn't find them. Frustrated, he abandoned the quest. "We must make an early start tomorrow. I'm off to bed."

He felt her gaze follow him from the room. Using all his self-control to keep from turning back, he climbed the stairs to the guest room, wondering why, if he was doing the honorable thing, he felt so miserable.

Chapter Eight

Rolling hills, barren and plowed for spring planting, homemade signs hawking pecans for sale and leafless trees, creating splotches of gray among the slash pines, shimmered in the late morning sun along the roadway choked with traffic headed south. Even in the enclosed space of the car with the heater throwing out warmth, Tory shuddered at the chill of the landscape.

She also suffered the chill of Rand's disposition. He'd been killing her with politeness ever since their pre-dawn breakfast. She'd probably offended his Victorian standards by her enthusiastic response to his kiss the night before. He must consider her—what was the old-fashioned term?—a brazen hussy.

He'd barely spoken then or during the two hundred miles they'd traveled since. He'd even seemed to lose his prodigious appetite. She groaned as both southbound lanes of traffic slowed ahead of them on the interstate. A delay wouldn't improve his already somber state of mind.

Beyond the crawling traffic where the road rose to an overpass, she spotted the orange and black markings of barriers across the road. "Detour ahead."

He shifted impatiently in his seat. "Are we in for a long delay?"

"Depends. Looks like they're routing us through Valdosta. If traffic's not too heavy, we might lose about fifteen minutes."

She'd been keenly aware of his restlessness since they'd left Atlanta. The slowness of their progress seemed to chafe at him, and although he seldom moved, she could gauge his restiveness by the occasional clench of his fists, the tightening of his lips and the abrupt shifting of his weight. Driving with him was like having a caged lion strapped into the passenger seat. And if he was this restless now, how agitated would he be in several days, when Smallwood's theories had proved to be empty promises?

Following the slow line of traffic ahead of her, she eased off the highway onto a country road. As they approached Valdosta, pine forest gave way to businesses and shops until they found themselves sandwiched between heavy traffic on a multilaned road.

"Victoria." He shifted toward her, and a quick glance confirmed that his expression matched the seriousness in his voice. "Come back with me."

His question threw her assessment of his mood into chaos. She'd considered his silence and aloofness a reproof of her conduct. But if he disapproved of her so strongly, why would he want her to accompany him?

She purposely misinterpreted his words. "Since I'm doing the driving, it seems I have little choice."

"Not to Florida." His tone caressed her, coaxed her. "Back to 1897. I have my private railcar. I'd show you Chicago, New York. We could even tour Europe together."

His invitation touched her, tempted her. "I can't accept your offer."

"Why?"

She shoved away last night's memories of her body beneath his, the heat of his lips against hers. They'd already caused her to lose most of her night's sleep. "Because what you ask isn't possible."

"Why not?"

She pressed the brake as the traffic light she approached flashed yellow. Caution, a good warning. She picked her words with care. "Because I don't believe in Smallwood's theories. In less than two weeks, you and I will be on this same road, headed in the opposite direction."

"But there's always the chance he's right. If another time shift does occur, would you go back with me?" He placed his hand over hers on the wheel, and for an instant she wondered if she could bear never feeling his touch again.

"Is this a proposal?"

His head snapped up, and he tightened his grip. "In a manner of speaking."

Her face flushed with pleasure and a rush of powerful affection until memories of Jill and her mother came to her rescue. "I don't belong in your time. Not only would I never see my sister again, but I couldn't fit the 1890s expectations of women."

"You'd exceed anyone's expectations." Admiration colored his voice.

She shook her head in denial. "I'm too self-sufficient, independent. Businesses in your day are owned and run by men for men. Do you know anyone who'd hire a woman to run their advertising campaigns?"

He said nothing but removed his hand from hers.

They rode on in silence interrupted only by the steady beat of the country station on the radio and the nasal twang of Conway Twitty. Traffic thinned and the road narrowed to two lanes, leaving the congestion of Valdosta behind for mile upon mile of slash pines, broken only by placid lakes filled with moss-draped cypress.

"This detour must be taking us the long way round," he complained.

"Unless I missed a turn back in Valdosta." She wouldn't be surprised. His almost-proposal had rattled her. "We'll stop at the next gas station and ask directions."

The narrow highway stretched on through uninhabited forest and wetlands. As the miles passed, she could feel Rand's tension building again beside her.

"Look, I'm sorry," she said. "I didn't delay us on purpose. Would you rather I turn around now and retrace the route through Valdosta?"

He pointed ahead to an ancient sign by the road. "Potts Store is only a mile. Stop there and inquire."

Within minutes she pulled into the gravel parking lot of a ramshackle building with fading paint. A rusted Dr. Pepper sign covered one side of the precarious structure, a post supporting the front overhang sagged, and peeling posters from a long-ago county fair flanked the screen door.

He gave a low whistle. "Beautiful."

"Huh?"

She shifted her gaze from the dilapidated structure to a shining chrome and metal motorcycle, the only other vehicle in the lot, while Rand surveyed the machine with the look of a starving man.

She reached across him and withdrew a map from the glove compartment. "I'll get directions. Sure you don't want something to eat?"

At the mention of food, he tore his gaze from the giant cycle, opened his door and followed her into the gloomy interior of the store.

As her eyes adjusted to the faint light, she observed tall shelves, jammed so closely together she had to turn sideways to sidle down the aisles. Layers of dust covered most of the merchandise.

He gathered up a bag of potato chips and a package of Ding-Dongs.

"Check their expiration dates," she warned, turning over a package to demonstrate. "Looks as if most of their inventory was here when Sherman passed through on his march to the sea."

She approached a tiny, grizzled woman behind the counter.

"Let me know if y'all don't find what you need." Snuff, packed inside the woman's lower lip, muffled her voice.

Tory opened her map and spread it on the counter. "We must have missed a turn back in Valdosta. What's the quickest route to I-75 south?"

"Oo-whee," the woman exclaimed with a grin. "Y'all are sure enough lost. You're headed due east." She stuck a shriveled finger at the map. "You best go on into Homerville and pick up 441 south. It'll connect you with the interstate at Lake City."

While Rand reimbursed the woman for his purchases, Tory took her bearings from the map, then drew a diet soda from an ancient cooler that clattered and banged like a mariachi band and paid the clerk. "Thanks for your help."

"Y'all come back," the woman called as Tory exited the store, squinting in the blinding light of the noonday sun. She popped the tab on her cola and drank thirstily.

Rand deposited his package in the car and stood admiring the giant Harley. "A magnificent machine. What wouldn't I give for one of those?"

The awe in his voice made her smile, remembering the adage that the only difference between men and boys was the size of their toys.

"Want to make a trade?" a raspy voice behind them asked.

She turned as a burly man dressed in black leather let the store's screen door slam behind him. He grinned at her as he picked his yellow teeth, glancing first at her, then at Rand, who'd ceased the study of the bike when the man spoke.

"No, thanks. Just looking." Rand crammed his hands in the back pockets of his jeans and gave the motorcycle one last covetous glance before opening the driver's door of the Toyota for her.

As she moved toward the car, the muscular man shot out a ham-size hand and grabbed her roughly by the wrist.

"I'll make you a good deal," he called to Rand. "Your car and your old lady for my hog."

She attempted to twist away, but the man held her fast.

"Let the lady go." Rand's voice, deadly calm, snapped across the parking lot.

"Think it over, man. You can always get another car, another broad." He jerked his head toward the bike. "But a custom-built machine like that one..."

She caught a glimpse of the man's dark, dilated pupils and wondered what drug he was high on. Stifling her rising hysteria, she spoke as calmly as she could. "It's my car, not his. Just do as he says and let me go."

Rand moved closer to them and the biker pulled a chain from his back pocket, twirling it until it circled his knuckles. The links glinted in the sunlight.

"Keep your car then," he sneered at Rand. "But your old lady is coming with me."

"She doesn't want to." Rand pulled his hands from his pockets and moved a step closer.

The man threw back his head and laughed, filling the air with the rancid stink of his breath. "What she wants ain't got nothing to do with it."

"Let the lady go."

She shivered at the menace in Rand's voice. Couldn't her captor hear it, or had drugs scrambled his hearing as well as his reason?

The biker dragged her closer.

Rand held up both hands, palms outward, and approached the biker. "All right. Let's talk. I might be willing to consider a trade after all."

She stared at him in disbelief. If he was bluffing, he gave no sign. The biker's grip tightened on her arm.

Behind her, the screen door slammed again. Glancing over her shoulder, she spied the clerk, standing on the steps of the building, nervously tugging a faded sweater over her shapeless cotton dress.

"Sanford Potts," the old woman called. "You been eating them mushrooms again?"

"Shut up, Ma," he yelled. "Go back inside and mind your store."

"What about it, Mr. Potts?" Rand stood just a few feet away, cool and contained in the noonday sun.

Tory could see herself and Potts reflected in the mirrored surface of Rand's sunglasses, but she couldn't see his eyes. She searched for signs of tension in his body, anything that might give her a clue to what he intended, but his powerful arms hung loosely at his sides and he distributed his weight lightly on both feet. If she judged by his body language, he could have been discussing something as trivial as the chance of rain.

Hell, she could wait all day for him to rescue her. She reached behind with her left foot, hooked it around the biker's ankle and yanked with all her might. With a howl, the heavy man tumbled into the dust, breaking his hold on her as he fell.

She sprinted for the car, past Rand, who stepped between her and the man on the ground. Potts shook his head like a wounded bull, wiped a meaty fist across his flushed face, then bellowed with anger. In an instant, he was on his feet, charging his considerable bulk head-on toward Rand.

"Run," she screamed. "Get in the car!"

Rand held his ground as the human battering ram bore down on him. Then, so quickly that if she'd blinked, she'd have missed it, Rand's right fist shot forward, catching Potts on the nose, lifting him off his feet, then dropping him into the dirt.

"You done killed him!" the old woman screeched, running on bandy legs toward her son's sprawled hulk. She knelt in the dust, cradled his head on her lap and fanned his face with her skirt.

Potts moaned and stared at his mother through unfocused eyes. "What happened?"

"He attacked you." She pulled a dingy handkerchief from her pocket and dabbed at his bleeding nose.

"On the contrary, Mrs. Potts. I saved your son from serious injury. Had I not stopped him, he would have rammed headfirst into Miss Caswell's automobile."

Rand knelt beside the biker and rummaged through his pockets.

"Hold on," Mrs. Potts said. "Do you mean to rob him, too? I'm calling the police."

"I wouldn't do that," Tory said. "They'll lock your son up for substance abuse."

Rand rose, brushed the dirt from the knee of his jeans and held up a set of keys that sparkled in the sunlight. "As soon as we've gone a mile, we'll place these at the foot of the next road sign."

He opened the door for Tory. Retroactive fear made her legs tremble and she welcomed the opportunity to sit as she eased behind the wheel.

"You all right?" he asked. "Want me to drive?"

"You?"

The corners of his mouth lifted in a jaunty grin. "I thought that would bring the color back to your face."

He closed her door, then circled the car and climbed in. As they exited the lot, she glanced at her rearview mirror. Mrs. Potts had her son by the ear, dragging his staggering bulk inside the store.

"If'n I told you once," the little woman hollered, "I told you a thousand times, them mushrooms'll fry what pea brain you got left."

"Leggo, Ma! Damn, you're hurtin' me!"

"You'll be lucky if I don't tan yore hide and hang it up to cure."

Tory headed east on the country road, stopping only long enough for Rand to deposit Potts's motorcycle keys beneath a speed limit sign. They rode on in silence until she could no longer curb her curiosity.

"Would you really have done a deal with Potts? Traded me for his cycle?"

He removed his sunglasses. "You interrupted the bargaining when you knocked Potts off his feet. He was in no mood for making a deal after that. I guess now we'll never know."

She caught a glimmer of humor in his eyes before he donned his glasses again, but whether it was good-natured or mocking, she couldn't tell.

RAND ADJUSTED his sunglasses on the bridge of his nose and hoped his eyes hadn't given him away. The mixture of rage and fear he'd experienced when the biker grabbed Victoria had shaken him worse than anything since the death of his parents.

Smallwood's theory had to work—and soon. Last night he'd conquered the urge to make love to her, to cradle her body against his and join himself to her flesh with violent tenderness. But earlier she'd made it clear she had no use for husband or family, and although the promiscuous attitudes of her society might excuse a casual sexual liaison, his own mores wouldn't allow him to indulge in such selfishness. When he committed himself to a woman, it would be for life. If Smallwood was right, his lifetime with Victoria would amount only to a matter of days.

He'd wanted her to return with him. He'd practically proposed marriage. But she had been right to refuse. Her world was too different from the one he'd left. She'd be a social outcast among his peers if she proclaimed her ideals of independence and self-sufficiency. Even the suffragettes didn't go that far.

Stay here with her. He disregarded the clamor in his heart. He'd be a misfit in her world. All he knew was making money, and he hadn't enough capital to build the kind of fortune to which he was accustomed. The thought of earning his living as an advertising symbol for other men's success galled him.

"Why are you so fascinated with motorcycles?" Her voice brought him out of his contemplation.

He considered her question a moment before answering. "Must be the power and freedom they provide."

"Like horses?"

"A horse has a will of its own that must be tamed to the rider's, but the machine would become an extension of oneself."

"Did you own one in Chicago? They did have them in 1897, didn't they?"

"I remember reading a newspaper article about Daimler in Germany building the first one, and now— in my time—some firm in Munich is manufacturing them commercially. But I doubt they're as sleek or powerful as what I've seen here."

"With the money you already have and what you'll make from the Money Man campaign, you can buy your own."

"When I return to my home in Chicago," he stated with emphasis, "I might purchase such a vehicle, but I doubt my horses will like it."

He pictured his stables, rows of magnificent animals who showed him more affection than most humans he knew. He'd cut short his stay at the Bellevue as soon as he'd consummated his agreement with Phiswick. He'd even purchase a motorcycle, although he doubted he'd be allowed to ride it on city streets. He concentrated on the deals he'd make after Phiswick, tallying his millions in his mind, attempting without success to forget the woman at his side.

"Lake City's just ahead," she said. "We'll arrive at the Bellevue in time for dinner in spite of the detour."

He leaned back in his seat and closed his eyes. They couldn't arrive quickly enough to suit him. He prayed the temporal disturbance would occur soon, before he succumbed completely to the distractions of the twentieth century—and most distracting of all was Victoria Caswell.

"WHAT DO YOU MEAN, you're not leaving this room?" Tory winced as her voice leapt an octave. Immediately upon reaching their suite at the Bellevue, Rand had plopped himself down and stated he'd not set foot outside again.

He leaned back on the sofa and clasped his hands behind his head, looking at her with that intractable expression she'd come to dread.

"I don't know how long I'll have when time folds back on itself again. I don't want to miss my chance." His reasonable tone infuriated her.

"How many times do I have to tell you? It's all theory. There's isn't going to *be* a chance." She took a deep breath and lowered her voice. "You're stuck here and you might as well make the most of it—instead of holing up in this room like a hermit."

As he leaned toward her a frown creased his face. "What about you?"

Tired of the argument, she rubbed her aching forehead. "I certainly don't intend to sit here waiting for something that isn't going to happen."

"That's not what I meant." His gaze locked with hers, and his daunting expression cooled her anger. "When the time shift occurs, if you're here, will you be thrown back to 1897 as well?"

She sighed and collapsed into the chair across from him, wondering if the gleam in his eyes was hope or perversity. "I don't think I need to worry about that."

"You ought to be concerned, unless you've changed your mind about accompanying me. I checked with Emma. There's still no other room available."

She eyed him warily. Was he trying to get rid of her? If so, he was bound for disappointment. She refused to let him out of her sight. After all, she'd started the production wheels rolling on the ad campaign, and she intended to stick with him like a burr on a dog until the work was completed.

He rose and crossed the room to kneel before her chair. When she refused to meet his gaze, he placed a finger beneath her chin and tilted her face toward his. "Why are you so angry?"

Because you don't love me enough to want to stay here with me. Because now that I've found you, I don't want to lose you.

Awareness descended on her like a mountain rockslide and rebellious tears formed in her eyes. "I'm scared there's the slightest chance Smallwood might be right. I couldn't bear never seeing you again."

A tear rolled down her cheek and he smoothed it away with his thumb. "You mustn't cry. We've known all along I don't belong in your world. And that you'd be miserable in mine."

Another tear pooled and raced down her jaw to her lip. His fingers brushed it away, leaving a fiery trace tingling in their path.

"I'm not worth your tears," he said. "I've caused you nothing but inconvenience since my arrival. Once you've settled back into your routine, you'll forget me."

She stared at him, burning the image of his dark hair, smoky eyes and lean, muscled body into her memory. "I'll never forget you."

She was making a fool of herself. He'd already made it clear he didn't want to stay with her.

He groaned like a man in mortal pain. "Don't look at me that way, Victoria. I can't be responsible—"

Pressing her fingertips against his lips, she turned his logic against him. "If you're right and all we have left together is a few more days, why waste them?"

He grasped her hand and buried his face in her palm. His lips nibbled against her skin. "This isn't fair to you."

She ran the fingers of her free hand through the silky thickness of his hair. "I'm not asking for a lifetime. Just for now."

Lean, strong hands cupped her face as he forced her to meet his eyes. "And if I cannot return to the past?"

"Then I'll help you find happiness here."

Alarm bells clanged in a distant segment of her mind, reminding her of how love had killed her mother, of her own desire for independence, of the risk of becoming involved with a man in her employ. But as he lowered his hands, skimming the column of her neck, grazing her shoulders, caressing her arms, the frantic pulse of her heart drowned out the chaos of her conscience. She swayed toward him, drawn by a force stronger than gravity, older than time.

When he climbed to his feet, she feared for an instant he would turn away, but he bent forward, lifting her in his arms and carrying her toward the sofa. She reveled in the pressure of his embrace and twined her arms around him, clasping the back of his neck, drawing his mouth to hers.

Her breath mingled with his, and Rand descended into a world of desire, where his codes of conduct and responsibility evaporated in primal heat. He covered the warmth of her mouth with his, teasing her lips apart, tasting, delving, devouring, cherishing her soft, pliant body.

Her fingers kneaded the muscles of his shoulders and back through the soft cotton of his shirt, firing his blood, hardening his groin with longing. He stared into eyes of seawater green, deep springs reflecting his desire.

"My God, Victoria," he breathed against the satin smoothness of her throat as he placed her on the sofa and lowered his body to hers.

"Prayer won't help you now." Her face lighted with humor—and something deeper that stoked the flames in his loins.

She entwined her legs with his, drew him closer and tumbled through an abundance of sensations, the musky scent of sandalwood, the taste of salt, the pressure of his lips, the hardness of his body crushed against her hips, the pounding of her pulses. She wanted nothing more than to hold on to him for all time.

As his hand slid beneath her blouse and brushed across her breasts, she gasped in pleasure and trembled in anticipation as he slowly unfastened buttons, thrusting the fabric aside. She arched her back while his hands fumbled with the clasp of her bra. When he beheld her half-naked form beneath him, she exulted in the worship in his eyes.

"I have never seen anyone as beautiful as you." His hands cupped her breasts, teasing the peaks with his thumbs, sending a tremor of delight through her. His eyes ignited like molten steel. "Does this please you?"

In silent response, her fingers gripped his shoulders and she arched her back again, offering herself to him, while his fingers worked their magic. He dipped his head and flicked her nipples with his tongue until her body writhed with pleasure.

With eager fingers she tugged his shirt from his slacks and pushed it over the broad muscles of his chest, pulling it over his head, baring his torso. He clasped her to him with a muffled cry, and the shock of his bare skin against her breasts sent rivers of heat cascading through her. His arms enfolded her, his mouth consumed her and she could think of nothing but her need for him.

Suddenly he grew still, then raised himself upon his elbows, gazing at her with pain-filled eyes. "I cannot do this, Victoria."

She shivered as the somber expression on his face quickly drenched her desire. "I don't understand. I thought you wanted me."

"More than anything on earth. But because I...value you, I cannot sully your reputation by making love to you, then deserting you."

The agony on his face convinced her of his sincerity, but that fact didn't ease her frustration. "I don't want to be valued."

How could she make him understand that what she wanted was to be loved, to feel the length of his naked flesh against hers, to open her body to him, to feel the shuddering ecstasy of his release and her own? But the seriousness of his expression dampened her hopes and her ardor, as well.

Suddenly cold, she wriggled beneath his weight and he lifted his body from hers and sat beside her. When she'd pulled her blouse over her shivering skin, he drew her into his arms once more.

"I can't change who I am." He stroked her hair with a gentle hand. "If I had continued, loved you as I wanted, I would have dishonored you forever. I care for you too deeply to shame you so."

"Oh, Rand." She snuggled against his bare chest and sighed with frustration. Damn his Victorian values. "Times have changed. Lovemaking isn't something a man does to a woman. It's something they both enjoy. You wouldn't have dishonored me." She turned her face to his. "You would have honored me greatly."

"I could never view it that way. We're from two different worlds, Victoria." He lowered his lips to hers in a tender, lingering kiss.

When she finally caught her breath again, she laid her hand against his cheek, caressing the rough stubble that darkened the strong line of his jaw. "Men and women haven't changed that much in a hundred years. Neither has love."

Love. The word thundered in her ears. She'd fallen in love with Randolph Trent. She burrowed deeper in his embrace, contemplating the future. Smallwood's theories would prove worthless, Rand could play the part of her Money Man and then the two of them could settle down for happily ever after in her big house in Atlanta.

"Love isn't possible for us," he whispered against her hair.

She drew back and searched his face, remembering the elusive Selena and wondering if there was something he hadn't told her. "Why not?"

"There's the slight matter of a century that will soon separate us," he reminded her.

"Oh, that." She relaxed in his arms. She'd had a momentary lapse of reason earlier, believing in the possibility that time would open up again and take him from her. But with her common sense restored, her fears vanished. Once he realized he was in the twentieth century to stay, he'd allow himself to love her. The thought sent waves of tingling warmth through her body, and she nestled closer against him.

His arms tightened around her. "Let's make every minute we have left together a celebration. I'll call room service and order the best dinner in the house—filet mignon and a magnum of champagne."

"And candlelight," she murmured, "and a roaring fire in the fireplace, even if we have to run the air-conditioning on high to counteract the heat."

"And flowers for you, a roomful of flowers." He brushed her eyelids, chin and tip of her nose with his lips before merging his mouth with hers.

She sighed with contentment. The idea of remaining sequestered with him in the hotel room for the next ten days grew very appealing. Ten days was too long a time for any man to resist temptation. Besides, events were unfolding in a most satisfactory sequence. As she realized he hadn't mentioned money once since their return to the Bellevue, a low laugh bubbled in her throat and she returned his kiss with enthusiasm.

A faint rustle penetrated her haze of happiness, the room suddenly chilled, and without looking, she knew Angelina had returned.

When she raised her head from Rand's embrace, the ghostly young woman stood in front of the bay window, wringing pale, slender hands and crying softly. This time she didn't speak, didn't acknowledge their presence in any way, but paced back and forth before the windows while silver tears streaked her cheeks and splotched the bodice of her blue silk gown.

Tory stood, buttoning her blouse, straightening her jeans, and Rand rose behind her, placing a protective arm around her shoulders.

"Angelina." Compared to her own happiness, the young woman's plight seemed even more poignant than before. "You can't go on like this."

Startled, Angelina ceased pacing and stared across the room in surprise. "I thought I was alone."

"You are alone." Tory kept her voice gentle but firm, hoping she could save the young woman's spirit from an eternity of desperate searching. "And you will always be alone until you accept that you're dead."

Tory traced through the fragments of her memory, attempting to recall what she'd learned about ghosts and haunted houses. She remembered a phrase she'd heard a psychic use in an exorcism she'd seen on television. "Go into the light, Angelina. Someone will meet you there, maybe even Jason Phiswick, and you'll no longer be alone."

Angelina clenched her silk skirts in both fists as if struggling to cling to the world she knew. "I can't go. I *won't* go without Jason."

Rand released Tory and stepped toward the ghost. "We've told you. Phiswick is dead, too."

"How can you say such horrible things? I won't listen any longer." Angelina turned her back to them and gazed out the window. In seconds, she disappeared.

Rand returned to Tory and pulled her into his arms. "I hate the thought of leaving you here alone with Angelina."

Angelina's misery tempered her earlier happiness, and Tory rested her head against his chest. "I don't think she'd ever harm me. But it's difficult to witness her pain night after night."

"If I return to 1897 in time," he said, "perhaps I can prevent her death and stop her torment."

She raised her face and smiled at him. His kindness touched her. "Did anyone ever tell you what a lovely man you are?"

He kissed the tip of her nose. "*Hungry* is the more appropriate word."

"Yes, I've seen evidence of your appetite."

"Have you forgotten our celebration?" He released her, crossed the room to the phone and placed the order for dinner, flowers and a fire. Then he returned and tugged her down onto the sofa next to him. "Now, where were we?"

She came into his arms as naturally as breathing. He wrapped his arms around her waist and drew her against him. Twilight deepened outside the windows, and shadows in the room lengthened.

The devil take his luck. Why did he find such a woman only to lose her?

"Shall I turn on a light?" he asked.

"No, let's wait for the candles." She traced a finger up and down the muscle of his forearm, distracting him from thoughts of food.

"I like the music," he muttered against her hair.

"What music?"

"Can't you hear it? I believe it's a waltz."

She pulled away from him, listening to the lilting strains of a Strauss melody echoing through the room. "Where's it coming from?"

He picked up the remote control. "Maybe it's the television."

"No, the TV's off, or you'd see a glow from the screen."

"The radio?"

She crossed the room and checked the radio by the bed. "It's off, too."

"Perhaps it's coming from the ballroom." He opened the door and stepped into the hallway, but when he left the room, the music faded, only to swell when he entered it again.

"Maybe it's Angelina," she said, "playing tricks on us."

He cocked his head, trying to locate the origin of the sound. "It seems to be coming from the closet. Do you have another radio in there?"

"It could be coming through the wall from next door."

He flung open the closet doors and blinked in surprise. The racks of clothing and shoes had disappeared. Facing him was an image of the room in which he now stood, identical except for the missing television, minibar and telephone.

"It's happened!" His voice vibrated with excitement. "Time has bent back on itself. This closet has become a portal back to my time."

"What?" She stood at his elbow, her shoulders stiff, her face drawn. "I don't believe it."

Remorse, regret, excitement, fear, love and loss flooded him. Loss. He pulled her into his arms. Now that this chance to return had come, his deals with Phiswick seemed less important. More important than anything was the woman in his arms.

But he'd known her only a few days. Selena he'd known for years and yet he'd never seen her betrayal coming. Could he give up everything he owned, everything familiar for Victoria Caswell? Would he live to regret an impetuous moment if he rejected his only chance to return to his own time?

"I must go back. I dare not stay." He pressed her close, savoring the warmth of her against him one last time.

She drew back, staring at him speechlessly with stunned disappointment clouding her eyes.

He had to go—and quickly. Not only might the time portal disappear, but if he hesitated, his resolve to leave might weaken. If he spent another hour with her, he couldn't leave. What was wrong with him that he wouldn't allow himself to trust someone again? He bent his head and kissed her deeply.

"I will love you for all time," he promised in a husky voice. Then he turned and stepped into another century.

WHEN RAND STEPPED through the closet doorway, he vanished, and the racks of clothes reappeared. Tory stared at the space where he had disappeared, numb with shock.

A rapping at the door brought her out of her trance and into pain, a ripping, searing sense of devastation.

"Go away," she called.

The knock sounded again. "Room service."

She choked on tears. Room service had brought dinner and flowers for a celebration that would never happen. Bitterness rose in her throat as she opened the door. Instead of the uniformed waiter she expected, she found Emma, looking like a cat who'd polished off the best cream. She barged into the room without being asked.

"Having a problem with your closet, are you?" the little woman asked.

Tory, still reeling with bewilderment and loss, nodded.

Emma proceeded to the closet doors and peered in. "There's the answer."

Tory followed and stared at the rows of clothing and shoes. She turned to the maid. "What do you know about all this?"

Emma stepped behind her. "Look."

When Tory viewed the closet once more, the clothing had disappeared again, and Rand stood opposite her in his hotel room, staring out the window with the look of a man who'd lost his soul.

"You've got to give him a hand, m'dear," Emma's voice rumbled in her ear. "He can't save Angelina by himself."

She wheeled and confronted Emma. "What are you talking about?"

"He's going to need your help," the little woman insisted.

"Oh, no—"

But before she could protest again, Emma's strong arms shoved her into the closet. As she stumbled into his room, Rand caught her. The time portal closed behind her.

She was trapped forever in the past.

Chapter Nine

Disoriented and angry, Tory grasped the bedpost as her knees buckled beneath her. Her brief journey through the portal had sapped her strength.

"You changed your mind?" Rand stared at her, raking his fingers through his hair and grinning like a man who'd won the lottery.

"I had some help," she muttered. "Emma."

"The maid?"

"She shoved me through after you. I've been suspicious of her from the first time we met. Every time our paths cross, disaster follows."

She tottered on unsteady legs to the sofa and sank gratefully into its cushioned depths. Her head ached from grappling with her dilemma. Although she'd fallen in love with Rand, it had been on her turf, her terms. She'd never really believed he'd leave her, that time would shift again. She hadn't considered in her wildest dreams returning to the nineteenth century to live out her life.

Her life. She fell onto her side and pulled a sofa cushion over her head. What kind of life would she have now? Caswell & Associates didn't exist, so she had no job. Her parents hadn't been born yet, so she had no family. Grief weighed like a boulder on her chest as she stifled a sob. She'd never see Jillie again.

And she had no money. Bitter laughter gurgled in her throat. She'd always worn her independence like a banner, but now she had no way to provide for herself, not even the basics of food, shelter and clothing.

Clothing. She sat up and considered her clothes. Snug, faded jeans, bikini panties and a white silk blouse—her entire wardrobe, all eminently unsuitable for 1897. She wiggled her bare toes. She hadn't even been wearing shoes when Emma shoved her through the closet.

"What's happening now?" Rand pointed to the wall where the time disturbance had occurred.

An area the size of a window faded and disappeared, just long enough for a pink bundle to come flying through and land at her feet.

She leapt from the sofa and flung herself at the wall. "Emma!"

He restrained her before she crashed into the wallpaper. "Have you lost your mind?"

She struggled until she realized the wall had coalesced into a solid structure once more, then collapsed against the reassuring warmth of his chest.

"Emma," she grumbled through gritted teeth. "She's the one behind all this. She could return me to the 1990s if she wanted."

He gripped her chin gently between his thumb and forefinger and tilted her face toward his. "Is that what you want? To go back?"

She stared into his eyes, swirls of gray smoke almost black with tenderness. Remembering how she'd felt in the few minutes she thought she'd lost him forever, she hesitated. She loved him. She didn't doubt it. What worried her was the inequality of their life together in his time. Women were second-class citizens there. She resented that fact, and her resentment would slowly erode her love for him, eating away at it like acid on metal.

"Yes. I must go back," she said. *But I want you to come with me.*

The elation Rand had experienced when Victoria appeared evaporated like mist beneath the morning sun. "So you didn't come of your own free will?"

Her eyes sparked with anger. "I told you, Emma pushed me!"

"And you don't love me enough to stay?" He tried to keep the pain from his voice.

She broke from his embrace and paced the room. "It isn't a question of love."

"If not love, what?" He shoved his hands into his back pockets, resisting the urge to grab her, crush her to him and never let go.

Her voice sounded frail, as if her courage failed her. "What am I supposed to do? I have no job, no income. How can I support myself?"

Fear replaced the anger in her expression, and tenderness welled up inside him. "You don't have to support yourself. I have wealth enough to give you every necessity and any luxury you desire."

Caring for her, giving her a home, dressing her in the finest clothes, fulfilling her every whim would satisfy him, providing him a delightful outlet for the millions he earned.

But his offer didn't seem to please her. She lifted her chin and stared at him with fierce pride. "I don't want to be dependent on you, on anyone. Besides, I *need* to work. It defines who I am."

Now was his chance to repay the kindness she'd shown him. For her own good, he'd offer options he knew she'd hate. Then she'd give in and allow him to provide for her. "I'll help you find work."

She blinked in surprise. "What kind of jobs are there for a woman?"

He settled beside her on the sofa and took her hands, turning them over and examining her smooth palms. "Women of your class don't work in my society."

"What about the other classes?"

"Some are seamstresses—"

"Forget that. I haven't sewn a stitch since home economics class in high school."

He rubbed the bridge of his nose thoughtfully. "Some work as cooks—"

"Without a microwave, I'm hopeless," she confessed with a sad laugh.

"Or as maids or factory workers, but I doubt if they earn enough to make them truly independent." He scowled at the thought of her standing long hours on an assembly line or kneeling to scrub floors.

"What about professional women?" she asked.

"There's only one kind of professional woman in my day," he admitted with a grin, "the world's oldest."

She managed a feeble smile. "Surely women serve as teachers or nurses?"

"Are you trained in nursing?" he asked, closing his hands around hers.

She shook her head.

"You might be able to teach, but often school boards insist that their teachers remain unmarried—and I have other plans for you." He lifted her hands to his lips and planted kisses lightly on her knuckles.

She tugged her hands away. "Then there's no hope of having my own advertising agency?"

He winced as his proposal fell on deaf ears. "You could have it. I told you I'd give you anything you want, and I meant it."

"Don't you understand?" she cried. "If you *give* it to me, I'm just as indebted to you as if I didn't work at all."

"I see." His mind raced, searching for solutions. "Then I could loan you the money to start your own agency."

Her eyes glowed with hope for the first time since she'd stumbled through the time portal. "I'd pay you back—every penny."

"Whether you could make a success of it in a society that frowns on women owning businesses is doubtful," honesty made him add.

For a moment she looked ready to burst into tears, then indignation lighted her face. "If I could get my hands on Emma, I'd wring her neck!"

"If Emma sent you here, she must have had a reason."

Victoria leaned down and picked up the rose bridesmaid dress and pink satin shoes Emma had flung through time. "She said you couldn't save Angelina by yourself."

He rubbed the stubble on his chin. "Now it all begins to make sense. Emma appears to you first, then Angelina's ghost shows up. Next I pop into the picture. Now we're both here together to prevent Angelina's accident."

"If it's not too late." She spread the dress across the bed, then settled into a chair.

Her jeans hugged her long, slender legs and rounded hips, and the peaks of her breasts thrust tantalizingly against her silk blouse. Tawny hair cascaded over one eye, framing the attractive curve of her face. She was the most exquisite woman he'd ever met, yet even now their happiness together seemed doomed. Whoever Emma was, she had a hell of a cruel streak.

"Perhaps if we do as Emma wishes, she'll send you back to the twentieth century." The words tore at his heart as he attempted to reassure her. He wanted more than anything to keep her with him forever, but the spark of hope in her eyes convinced him his desire was futile.

"Then we'd better get started," she said. "If I'm missing from the hotel for long, the management will call the police. How will I explain where I've been?"

"First, you'll need a room."

"Why not share? Our arrangement worked out all right before." Her smile skewered him with longing.

"Times have changed, as the saying goes. If you are to associate with young Angelina, you must appear as a woman of impeccable character."

"And single women of impeccable character don't share rooms with men." She sighed and leaned her head against the chair, closing her eyes in resignation.

Marriage would solve a number of problems, but he didn't want Victoria tied to him as a matter of convenience. If ever they married, it must be because of love. Since she'd expressed the desire to return to her time, she obviously thought she could get along without him just fine.

But she was here with him now. And although she wasn't happy with the arrangement, just having her near him made his spirits soar.

He opened the closet and drew out his clothes—jodhpurs, riding boots and a white shirt. "I'd better change before someone sees me in these jeans and running shoes. They'd be difficult to explain.''

When he returned from the bathroom in his riding attire, she sat where he'd left her, staring at the wall where the time portal had opened earlier.

Her eyes widened when she saw him. ''I dreamed of you before we met. You were dressed exactly as you are now.''

A faint tinge of pink stained her cheekbones, and the strength of his desire to press his lips there almost strangled him. He moved toward the door.

''Why don't you change into something more suitable?'' He nodded toward the dress on the bed. ''I'll arrange for your room with the front desk.''

''Wait.''

She stood, stuffing her hands in the back pockets of her jeans, oblivious that her stance drew her shirt tighter across her breasts. Rubbing one foot against the back of her jeans leg, she raked her hair off her face with her fingers. ''Who am I supposed to be?''

She had a point. Why would a young, single woman, unchaperoned, be staying at the Bellevue?

He considered several possibilities before deciding on the most convincing. ''We'll say you're my cousin from Atlanta, here to recover from the untimely death of your parents. I'll see what I can do about locating a chaperon.''

''Chaperon? I haven't been chaperoned since my junior high prom.'' Her face flushed with resentment.

He tried, but couldn't restrain the grin that split his face. "Welcome, Miss Caswell, to 1897."

As the door closed behind him, she turned to remove her clothes, but the view beyond the window caught her eye. Even in the deepening darkness, she could distinguish the edge of the bluff, dipping to the gulf. Not a condominium or hotel anywhere in sight. Night herons skittered along the tidal flats, and black skimmers swept low over the gently breaking surf. The stars shone brightly in the western sky, unmuted by city lights. The loneliness of the deserted landscape chilled her, reminding her how much she'd lost.

But you'll always have Rand.

She pushed the seductive thought away as she shucked her shirt and jeans. She floated the pink satin over her head, thankful the dress was fully lined with attached petticoats. Even so, if any Victorian ladies caught sight of her bare legs beneath her hems, they'd probably swoon with righteous outrage. Once she'd checked into the room Rand found for her, she'd have to hole up until she could acquire the necessary clothing.

Turning to the mirror over the bureau, she attempted to arrange her hair in an appropriate style, racking her memory for Gibson Girl details.

"I've booked you into 128, a suite across the hall," Rand announced upon his return. "I was lucky they had a vacancy so close."

She turned to him and brushed back a curl falling in her eyes for lack of hairpins. "A room will help, but I'll be stuck there unless you can arrange for additional clothing for me. I'll cause a small scandal if I appear anywhere in public looking like a refugee."

Refugee. The word rang in her ears as she realized the seriousness of her plight, stranded in a strange time in a strange land, knowing no one but the man before her.

As his gaze raked her from head to foot, she thrust a bare ankle into view, twirling it like a cancan dancer. "See what I mean?"

His steely eyes stopped her. "I won't be responsible for my actions if you continue that."

She raised her skirt higher. "You've seen me in much less."

With two broad steps, he crossed the room, reached out and dragged her to him, crushing her against his chest. His hand grasped the back of her neck, drawing her lips to his, while his other hand crushed the satin of her bodice.

She gasped at the furor of his kiss, inhaling his scent of sunshine and sandalwood. As she twined her fingers in his hair, she strained toward him, feeling the hardness of his body through layers of petticoats. And her response had nothing to do with her dependence on him.

Abruptly, he pulled away, holding her by the shoulders at arm's length. The gravity of his expression frightened her. "We must live by a different code now. My society is much different from what you're accustomed to."

His chastising tone brought back thoughts of women's place in his time. Her temper flared. "Don't lecture me."

He brushed her lips lightly with his own. "Not a lecture, just a friendly reminder. I want to spare you any embarrassment."

Her resentment faded. She touched a hand to her lips, swollen from the pressure of his mouth. More than anything she wanted to stay with him, to crawl between the sheets of the wide poster bed with him and never leave the room, never worry about social mores or bare ankles or chaperons—or Angelina.

When he dropped his hands and moved away from her, she knew she would have to play by his rules. "What am I to do about my clothes?"

He smiled a slow grin that assured her he wasn't angry. "I told the concierge the railroad had lost your trunks. He said he would contact a seamstress in the village to see what can be done."

"Thank you." She felt grateful and helpless at the same time, and she hated the feeling.

The voices of people passing in the corridor brought a look of alarm to his face, and he dug into his pocket and fished out a key. "You must go to your room before anyone sees or hears you here."

She glared at him, despising his Victorian rules.

He brushed back a lock of hair that had spilled over her eye. "It's for your sake. It is always the woman whose reputation is harmed."

"It's called a double standard in my time," she muttered.

He opened the door, peered up and down the hallway, then motioned for her to follow. They hurried the dozen yards to Room 128 unobserved. When he lifted the key to the lock, the door swung open. Emma stood there, dressed in a black taffeta dress and a black lace cap.

"You!" Tory sputtered with anger. "This is all your fault!"

"Don't just stand there gawking, m'dear. Come in and welcome your dear aunt Emma, who's come all the way from Savannah to stay with you." Her long skirts rustled as she stood aside for them to enter. "You, too, young man. Now that I'm here, you're properly chaperoned."

Tory shivered at the menace in Rand's expression as he scowled at Emma. "You owe us an explanation, and it had better be good."

Undaunted, Emma pointed to a table beneath the windows. "You haven't had your dinner yet, so I've arranged for tea and sandwiches."

Tory followed Rand inside, but a rumbling in the hallway distracted them. Emma opened the door wider and stood aside for the bell captain, who pushed a loaded luggage cart into the room.

"Miss Caswell?" he asked.

"I'm Miss Caswell." Tory stepped forward, eyeing the gleaming leather and brass-bound steamer trunks the man hefted from his cart onto the Oriental carpet.

"The desk sent these up. Said the railroad located your luggage and apologizes for the inconvenience."

Her mouth fell open in surprise. "My luggage? But—"

"How efficient." Emma beamed a smile at the bellman and lifted an eyebrow in warning to Tory. "My niece is delighted her wardrobe has been recovered."

Rand dug into his pocket for a coin and tipped the porter, who responded with a jaunty salute before dragging his empty cart away.

When he'd closed the door behind the man, Rand turned to Emma. Anger glinted in his steel gray eyes and contracted the muscles of his jaw. "What's the meaning of this?"

Emma bent over the first trunk and lifted the lid, exposing elegant dresses packed in tissue paper. "You can't expect Victoria to live among the wealthy of the Bellevue without a proper wardrobe." When Rand began to protest, she raised her hands. "I know, Mr. Trent, eventually, you would have provided her with all she needed. I've simply saved you both a great deal of time and embarrassment."

Dazed and mystified, Tory sank into the nearest chair. "But how—"

Emma motioned to the chair across the table from Tory. "If you'll take a seat, Mr. Trent, I'll explain everything from the beginning."

He sat stiffly and folded his arms across his chest, glaring at Emma with undisguised hostility. "If you're the one responsible for bouncing us back and forth in time, disrupting our lives, your explanation had better be damned good."

"How do you do all this?" Tory's gesture encompassed the room and overflowing trunks. "Who are you?"

Emma, seemingly unintimidated by Rand's anger and Tory's questions, poured tea from a silver pot and removed a damask napkin from a plate of sandwiches. "Beings such as myself are called many things—guardian angels, fairy godmothers—"

"Right." Tory smirked. "As in bippety-boppety-boo?"

Rand's frown deepened. "Bippety-boppety—"

"The magic incantation of Cinderella's fairy godmother," Tory explained.

"A dreadful stereotype." Emma pursed her lips in disapproval. "However, I prefer the term *facilitator*. It's much more up-to-date, more accurate, too."

She carried her cup and saucer to the sofa opposite them and spread her taffeta skirts around her, exposing the tips of small black boots.

"Ridiculous," Rand scoffed. "There's no such thing."

"Your attitude is to be expected. We are instructed never, if possible, to make our presence known." Emma sipped her tea daintily. "However, in this case, I've been given special dispensation."

"This case?" Tory asked.

"Angelina Fairchild. That girl, whom I watched over diligently until she reached the age of twenty, had been assigned to my care." Emma's brow puckered thoughtfully and she ducked to set her cup on the coffee table, but not before Tory spotted glistening tears in her eyes. "Unfortunately, my care proved inadequate."

Tory experienced a twinge of sympathy for the little woman and her obvious distress over Angelina's death. "After Angelina's death, then what did you do?"

Aware of Rand's stiff posture across from her, Tory avoided his disapproving gaze.

"What happened to me is unimportant," Emma said. "Call it a mid-life crisis if you wish, but I blotted my copybook—"

"Huh?" Tory's forehead creased at the unfamiliar phrase.

"Screwed up, I believe, is the indelicate way your generation puts it." Emma leaned back against the sofa. "I was supposed to protect Angelina, who should have lived a long and happy life, but I was...distracted, and she died." Emma withdrew a lace handkerchief from her sleeve and dabbed her eyes.

"I don't understand what this has to do with us." Rand's voice softened, but his fierce expression remained.

"It's a bit complicated." Emma tucked her handkerchief into her cuff, patted the lace ruffles of her cap and folded her hands in her lap. "Facilitators have great powers, but dominion over life and death is denied us. We use the powers we have to expedite a birth or prevent a death, but once a person dies, we cannot bring them back."

"So there's no hope for Angelina?" Tory asked.

"Under normal circumstances, no," Emma said, "but Angelina's distress, her unplanned pregnancy, her refusal to leave this world once her body died have created a tragic, unhappy situation, I've been given special permission to attempt to reverse her death."

"You still haven't explained how we're involved in this," Rand said.

Emma's plump fingers twisted the folds of her skirt. "Although my Superior will not permit me to intervene personally to prevent Angelina's accident, I am allowed to enlist two mortals to save Angelina's life."

Rand's eyes narrowed. "I understand why you've chosen me. I know Angelina and her lover. But why drag Victoria back a hundred years?"

Emma sighed. "That was part of the deal."

"Deal?" Tory asked. "I don't understand."

"To allow me to regain my standing—and more importantly, to save Angelina—my Superior insisted I make a trade."

"Hold on." Rand jumped to his feet and moved to Tory's side, placing an arm around her shoulders like a shield. "If a trade means swapping our lives for Angelina's, you can forget it."

"You're right in one sense, Mr. Trent," Emma said. "But I'm not asking for your deaths. Only that you exchange the lives you have for new ones."

"I'm sorry for Angelina's torment," Tory said, "but I like the life I have just fine, thank you."

Emma shook her head sadly. "My Superior says Angelina can be saved only if I find two people whose lives are headed for irredeemable unhappiness. If I can persuade them to assist me, Angelina will be saved, and they will be happier in the bargain. You, m'dears, are those two."

"Of all the insulting—" Rand choked with rage, and as he drew closer, the muscles of his thighs tensed against Tory. "Who are you to say we're headed for irredeemable unhappiness?"

Emma's lavender eyes flashed, and Tory shuddered when she glimpsed an intractable will behind the plump little maid's facade.

"I come not only from your future, Randolph Trent, but from Tory's, as well. I know how both your lives will play out." Emma stood and paced before them, and the rustling of her skirts accompanied her words. "You both are so consumed by your work, so removed from other people, I had to drug you to get your attention."

Rand remembered the night of his meeting with Phiswick and the hotel maid who kept refilling his glass. "You were here before—"

Emma nodded. "I'm the one who placed you in Tory's bed."

"And drugged my tea so I'd dream of him and not awaken until you'd put him there," Tory added.

"And doctored your drinks and coffee at the Bellevue and the wine I left in Atlanta. Once I broke your initial preoccupation with making money—" she nodded to him "—and avoiding commitment—" she looked at Tory ''—your natural instincts took over and drugs were no longer necessary.''

''How dare you manipulate our lives?'' Tory snapped.

Emma's wise gaze pierced them both. ''Can you honestly tell me you wish you'd never met each other?''

Rand tightened his hand on Tory's shoulder, and she covered it with her own. Neither spoke.

''Just as I thought.'' Emma nodded with a self-satisfied air. ''It would have been much simpler if I could have found two people in the same time period who fit the requirements, but at least my Superior allowed me limited access to temporal disturbances to achieve my goals.''

Tory's head lifted and alarm glimmered in her eyes. ''*Limited* access?''

Rand considered life without Victoria, and the knot in his chest made speech difficult. ''If she helps save Angelina, will you return her where she belongs?''

''I have one time passage left,'' Emma said. ''I can send her back once Angelina is safe.''

If he refused to help Angelina, he could keep Victoria with him. The thought tempted him—until he realized any happiness they found would be built upon Angelina's torment. And would Victoria ever forgive him if he ruined her one chance to return to her own time?

''What do we have to do?'' he asked.

"Tonight is Thursday," Emma said. "Saturday will be the day Angelina dies. You can begin by canceling your meeting for that day with Jason Phiswick."

He contemplated his future. How could Emma believe she would redeem him from unhappiness without Victoria? Until Victoria had shown him what love could be, he hadn't realized how lonely and unhappy his life had been.

He studied the woman beside him, who appeared uncomfortable and overdressed in her stylish gown. Her golden hair tumbled haphazardly from the coronet she'd attempted to fashion in the style of his day. Attempting to live as a stiff and proper lady would make her miserable. She was too accustomed to her freedom and independence, going her own way without assistance, wearing delectably few clothes, heading her own business. The customs of his day would stifle her, condemning her to a slow, unhappy death.

Blast Emma and her busybody facilitating! In her attempt to rescue him from his unhappy life, she'd succeeded only in calling attention to how miserable he really was. Victoria, at least, had a chance for happiness—if they did as Emma said and saved Angelina, so the little woman would send Victoria forward in time where she belonged.

"I'll tell Phiswick tomorrow that the meeting has to be postponed," he promised.

"And you?" Emma turned her amethyst gaze on Victoria.

Ignoring Emma, Victoria raised her head and stared at him. The love reflected in her face deepened his torment at the thought of losing her forever. He steeled himself and answered for her. "Of course she'll help. She wants her own life back—the sooner the better."

The sooner the better. If she stayed too long, he might not let her leave.

Chapter Ten

Tory's foot caught in the train of her riding habit and she stumbled. If Rand hadn't grabbed her by the waist, she would have pitched headfirst down the broad stairway. The pressure of his arms around her was the only compensation for the torture of nineteenth-century fashion.

"Thanks." She smiled at the look of alarm on his face. "I might have broken my neck."

With a well-placed kick and a stifled curse, she knocked the voluminous train behind her and adjusted the flowing veil that secured the hard-crowned hat to her head. "I'm wearing enough fabric to clothe a small army—and everything in depressing black. Mourning, Emma calls it."

His lips curved upward in response, but he seemed preoccupied and the strong planes of his face glowed pale in the brilliant morning sun streaming through the windows of the landing.

"Are you okay?" she asked.

When they descended into the crowded lobby, he tucked her arm more firmly through his. "I'm fine, although I had some trouble sleeping—alone."

She reveled in the fact that he'd missed her. "You're lucky you didn't have Emma snoring away in the next room."

"Where is our facilitator now?"

"Once she laced me into this straitjacket and skewered my head with pins, she disappeared." She stopped to breathe but could take in little air against the strictures of her whalebone stays. "No wonder the women of your era are so repressed. Their clothes hold them prisoners."

She booted her skirts again, drawing a disapproving frown from an ample-bosomed matron. The older woman's censure turned to blushes of pleasure when Rand tipped his hat and greeted her by name as they passed.

He bent and spoke softly in Tory's ear. "A gallop in the fresh air will make you feel less like a captive. I've requested a gentle mount for you."

"Fresh air won't help if I can't breathe," she grumbled, wishing for a T-shirt and shorts. Her foot twisted on the high heel of her boot and she longed for sneakers, as well.

"You were much sweeter tempered when you were sleeping with me," he observed. "Perhaps we should return to our former arrangement."

"That suits me fine—as long as we return to the 1990s." She stepped onto the wide veranda and looked east across the golf course.

"Mr. Trent! How nice to see you. You've been gone for several days."

A warm, bubbling voice drew her attention from the wilderness, which stretched inland from the hotel grounds, to Angelina Fairchild, who approached them on the porch twirling a lavender parasol that matched her stylish gown. Vibrant color flushed her cheeks, and the hand she extended at Rand's introduction gripped Tory's warmly.

"I'm delighted to meet you, Miss Caswell." Her heart-shaped face lighted with animation. "Will you and Mr. Trent join us at our table for dinner this evening? Mama is gathering a small group for the meal and a soiree afterward."

The attractive, vivacious girl held little resemblance to the tortured spirit Tory had met before. She considered the purpose of her journey back in time. If she was to prevent Angelina's death, she must become better acquainted with her. After a confirming nod from Rand, she presented the young woman with her best smile. "We'd love to have dinner with you, Miss Fairchild."

Angelina inclined her head, stirring the egret plumes on her wide-brimmed hat, and strolled gracefully away, unencumbered by her restricting skirts.

When Tory descended the veranda stairs, her boots tangled in her skirts. With a savage wrench, she freed them.

"I like Angelina." She attempted to match her steps to Rand's long stride. "I hope we can prevent her accident."

"So you can return to your time?"

"Because she deserves better," she insisted.

The broad brim of his hat hid his expression, but the emotionless tone of his question nagged at her. How could she make him understand she couldn't stay, that the restrictions of his time would suffocate her and destroy their love?

Her foot caught again and she grabbed his arm like a drowning sailor clasps a lifeline. A lifeline. That's what he was. Without him, her life wasn't worth— She closed her mind against the expletive. In this time and place, proper young women didn't even *think* such words.

She attempted to keep her voice light. "I hope my horse has steadier legs than I do, or I may never see the twentieth century again."

"You're worried about your Money Man campaign, aren't you? And what will happen when I don't return?" His bland tone frightened her, as if a stranger spoke from beneath the shadow of his hat.

"No."

She kept her voice as colorless as his, afraid to disclose how strongly she felt about losing him, afraid he'd try to keep her there. Afraid she'd want to stay.

But she had spoken the truth about her ad campaign. To hell with the Money Man. Her assistants could scour the country, using Rand as a standard, and come up with a suitable model for Benson, Jurgen and Ives. But where would she ever find a man who made her senses reel, who cherished her as Rand did?

A groom led two horses into the stable yard, a chestnut stallion that danced against the bit and a docile gray mare.

"The gray's yours," Rand said. "Would you like a hand up?"

She eyed the gentle beast warily. She'd ridden only a few times before at a riding academy in the country when she was a teenager. The back of the small gray looked a long way from the ground.

"What's that scrap of leather it's wearing?" she asked.

He pushed back his hat with the tip of his index finger and grinned at her. "That's a saddle."

"No." She shook her head and pointed to the chestnut. "Your horse has a saddle. Mine doesn't."

"It's a sidesaddle." Amusement glinted in his flint gray eyes. "A lady always uses a sidesaddle."

She studied the unfamiliar equipment, then tugged at her soft leather gloves. "I'll need some help."

His strong hands spanned her waist as he lifted her onto her precarious perch. "Hook your leg around the saddle horn. It'll hold you steady."

"That's easy for you to say." She swayed on the horse's back as she arranged the train of her habit across its rump. "God, I miss my Toyota."

"Toyota?" asked the groom holding her reins.

"My own little gray." She attempted a smile in the haughty fashion of a Victorian lady. "You'd be amazed at the horsepower—"

"Victoria," Rand warned.

"Sorry."

She should have known better. She'd watched enough "Star Trek" to know one mustn't do anything to change the course of history when one travels through time. Just the thought made her roll her eyes skyward while she doubted her sanity. Surely she'd awaken soon in her own comfortable bed at the Bellevue to discover this had all been a crazy dream.

Rand placed a foot in the stirrup and mounted with the fluid grace of long practice. Leaning down, he accepted a pair of wicker hampers from the groom and slung them before him.

"A picnic." He nodded toward the baskets. "I thought we'd make a day of it."

She smiled. "I should have known you wouldn't go far without food."

"It won't be filet mignon and candlelight, but there is champagne." His expression made eloquent promises of things to come, sending the butterflies in her stomach into kamikaze dives. He dug his heels into his horse's flanks and moved out of the stable, heading south, and she urged her horse cautiously behind him.

He reined in his mount to a slow walk, and she had no problems with her gray. They followed a trail that skirted the golf course, then entered a thick pine forest. The resinous scent of pine mixed with the salty tang of the gulf, the sun shone brighter, the sky burned bluer and the wind blew fresher than she'd ever experienced. Was the perfection of the day due to the absence of twentieth-century pollution or had the man at her side heightened her awareness?

"We have a problem," Rand announced.

She pulled her gaze from the scenery. "Only one?"

"I spoke with Jason Phiswick this morning and told him our Saturday meeting was canceled."

"So what's the problem?"

"I did too good a job selling him on my proposal. He insists on meeting. Says the whole deal is off unless we meet as planned."

She tugged at the reins, hauling her horse to a halt. "What now?"

"Instead of meeting with him, I'll join you in keeping an eye on Angelina. Perhaps, between the two of us, we can keep her safe until she tells Jason about their child."

She shifted on her saddle. "What if he's not happy about impending fatherhood?"

"Phiswick is an honorable man. He'll do the right thing."

Rand indicated a narrow trail through the trees, descending to the bay where the outgoing tide left the flats exposed. She flicked the reins and followed him onto the wet sands, where great blue herons, white ibis and roseate spoonbills scattered at their approach.

Over deeper waters, squadrons of brown pelicans swooped and dived and the silver flash of mullet broke the rippled surface of the bay.

She inhaled the invigorating salty scent. "I can't believe how clear and clean the air is."

A cynical smile lifted a corner of his mouth. "At least there's one thing about my time that you approve of."

"It's not a question of approval. I just don't belong here. I'd never fit in. If I were a man, it might be easier—"

Rand reached out and placed his hand over hers on the reins. "If you were a man, I wouldn't care if you stayed or not."

His smoldering expression ignited a responsive flare within her. "If I were a man, Randolph Trent, I might beat you at your own moneymaking game."

"I'd give every cent I own if you could stay here with me and be happy." He squeezed her fingers gently, and she despised the gloves that deprived her of the feel of his skin against hers.

"Even the magical Emma can't grant us that," she said with a sigh.

"Then we must make the most of the time we have." He pointed to an oak grove on the bluff above the bay. "The perfect spot for a picnic."

RAND SECURED the reins of his horse to a low branch and turned to assist Victoria in dismounting. He grasped her waist as she leaned down, but her skirt tangled in the stirrup and she fell toward him. The length of her body slid against his, and even through layers of fabric and unyielding stays, he could detect every soft, delectable curve.

His yearning for her, born the day he'd awakened in her bed, coursed through him with new life at her touch. His heart pounded against his ribs, threatening to burst from the strength of his emotion. He swallowed the bitter irony that now he'd learned to love, he'd soon lose forever the woman who'd freed him from his lonely, loveless existence.

Her hands grasped his shoulders for support, and he felt himself drowning in the depth of her sea green eyes. When he bent to kiss her, swaths of veiling and the brim of her riding hat blocked his way.

She pushed him back with a musical laugh. "First I'm going to get rid of all this."

"All what?" His mouth went dry.

"You'll see." She swung the heavy train of her habit over one arm and pirouetted in the shady clearing beneath the oaks. "There isn't another human being for miles, so I can be myself without worrying about the approval of your Victorian contemporaries."

Her declaration shocked and excited him. He delighted in her independence, her rejection of the constraints of his society, her free spirit; but all the qualities that made him love her were the very traits that prevented her happiness in his world.

"Will *I* approve?" he asked with a teasing grin.

Untying her veils, she tossed her hat aside and confronted him with glowing eyes. "You're definitely going to approve."

While she tugged off her gloves, he removed the wicker baskets from his horse, took a tartan from one of them and spread it beneath the oaks.

She settled on the blanket and lifted one foot, exposing a shapely leg encased in a black stocking. "I'll need some help with these boots."

Instinctively his body responded as, with his back to her, he straddled her leg and gripped her small boot in his hands. She braced her other foot against his backside as he yanked off first one boot, then the other. When he turned to face her, she lay back on her elbows with a smile of invitation and acceptance and a warmth that melted his heart. Falling to his knees, he gathered her in his arms.

His lips moved against her hair, nibbled at her earlobe, traced the curve of her cheek. As he kissed the pulsing vein at her throat, savoring the salt and sweetness of her skin, her quivering response stoked the fires of his passion. Cradling her face in his hands, he drew back, devouring her with his gaze.

"How can I live without you, Victoria?"

She placed her small hands over his and gently pushed them away. "We must store up memories, enough for a lifetime."

While he reclined on one elbow, her agile fingers, unfastening the covered buttons of her riding jacket, mesmerized him. She sketched his mouth with a fingertip, then laid her jacket aside and struggled with the waistband of her skirt. When it sprang apart, she rose to her feet, stepped out of the voluminous garment, tossed it across a low branch and turned back to him with a smoldering look.

Tension built within him as she unwound the white stock at her throat and shrugged off her blouse. His body ached from the pressure of his longing when her petticoats fell in a mound around her feet.

She sank beside him and turned her back, pointing to the laces of the corset that nipped her waist and thrust her breasts upward.

"Our Emma must be something of a sadist," she grumbled. "I haven't been able to breathe since she laced me into this thing this morning."

He fumbled with the laces with fingers stiff as fence posts. As the stays fell away, her sigh of relief rocked him with tremors of delight. Clasping her back to his chest and nuzzling aside the straps of her shift to kiss her shoulders, he drew her to him. Through the thin linen, her breasts pressed against his forearm, where his pulse hammered against her heart.

When she spoke, the breeze caught her words and flung them away from him.

His lips moved against her ear. "What did you say?"

With her eyes glowing like sunlight on water, she turned to face him. "I love you, Randolph Trent. No matter where—or when—I am, I will always love you."

His chest tightened with tenderness until he could hardly speak. "Always is a long time."

She rested her forehead against his chin. "By this time next week, I will have loved you for almost a hundred years."

Thrusting away thoughts of a future without her in his arms, he groaned and buried his fingers in her thick, honeyed hair. One by one he withdrew the offending hairpins until her tresses tumbled free about her flushed face.

When she lifted moist, eager lips to him, he crushed his mouth to hers, mingling their breath. Her heart thudded against his ribs, driving the air from his lungs, while her hands slipped up his chest, opening his shirt, pulling it from his shoulders.

Panting for breath, he raised his head. Blue green eyes met his.

"Don't stop, please," she murmured.

He could barely hear the words, soft puffs of breath against his cheek.

"I need you." Her faint voice sounded thick with desire.

"God knows, I do not want to stop."

"Then don't."

As he bent to kiss her once more, she caressed the muscles of his arms with light, feathery strokes, ran her fingers playfully down his chest, then dipped her hands lower.

"I must seem bold and brash compared to the women you know," she stated with characteristic bluntness.

"To be honest—" he raised an eyebrow and assumed a serious face "—I like bold women."

At his statement, she grew still. "Have you known many?"

"Just one. And I'd like to know her better."

Her laughter, a crystalline sound like water bubbling over rocks, broke the quietness of the oak grove. "I think that can be arranged."

Every nerve hummed with desire and he restrained himself from taking her there and then.

"There's an old Chinese proverb that says, 'May you receive what you wish for.'" Her gaze never wavered, although a tinge of pink darkened the ridges of her cheeks. She drew up her knees and rolled her stockings down her calves and over trim ankles, drawing them off in a slow, sensuous gesture that almost shattered his restraint.

"We have too little time to waste on decorum." He grasped the hem of her chemise and tugged it over her head, freeing her breasts. Red welts from her corsets crisscrossed her skin and he smoothed them with his fingers in slow, languorous circles.

As she pressed against him, the hardened nubs of her nipples seared his skin, and she dropped her hands to his jodhpurs and undid the buttons.

Mischief gleamed in her eyes as she freed him of his boots and trousers. "I doubt the late Queen Victoria would approve of my behavior."

The gulf breeze flowed over his bare skin but had no cooling effect on his ardor. Loosening the drawstring at her waist, he gently stripped away the last of her garments. "She would advise you to lie back and think of England," he teased.

"You are all I can think of now." She trailed her hands down the indentation of his spine, drawing him to her.

Beneath him, her tanned body glowed golden in a shaft of sunlight spilling through the branches. Dear God, he loved this woman, loved her enough to spend the rest of his days with her and cherish her every minute of them. But in a matter of days, perhaps only hours, Victoria would be lost to him for all time.

He poised above her, rigid with desire, longing to enter her with one sure, powerful thrust, to claim her as his own, yet fearful of sending her back to the future carrying his child.

As if she'd read his mind, she brushed his cheek with the back of her hand. "I won't get pregnant. I told you, the women of my time know how to prevent it."

The lie came easily to her lips. If he wouldn't return with her, at least, with any luck, she might have his child, a reminder always of the only man she'd ever loved.

As he caressed the warm, moist heat of her, all thought of past and future disappeared, vanquished by his touch. Pleasure erupted like fire, flowing through her veins, consuming her in its blaze.

He lowered his hips to hers and she gasped when he entered her. Clasping him closer, she tightened her body around him, ascending to a height of awareness that blocked all sensation but the pulsing thrust of him.

For one instant time stopped, the sun stood still, the wind held its breath. Deep within the core of her, electricity exploded, jolting her with its intensity, and the only sound was her voice blending with his as they plummeted together into forever.

DRESSED in her shift, Tory leaned against the rough bark of the oak, watching Rand unpack the basket the hotel chef had prepared for them. She wished she had a camera to capture the look of him—tousled hair, bare feet, breeches only partly buttoned, riding low on his narrow hips. Would she remember the scent, the feel of him when she returned to her own time? Her hunger for him began to build once more.

He removed a bottle of champagne from an oilcloth bag filled with cracked ice, then worked the cork loose.

After pouring the bubbling liquid into crystal flutes and handing her a glass, he sat beside her.

"A toast." He raised his glass. "To the woman I love."

She raised the wine to her lips, but she couldn't drink with emotion closing her throat. She blinked away tears. "Ask Emma to send you back with me."

He set his glass aside and reclined with his head in her lap. "You know that wouldn't work."

She laced her fingers through his thick, fine hair. "Why not? Men enjoy the same rights and privileges in my time that they do in yours."

"There's a difference. Because I'm accustomed to women's dependency, I believe a man must support the woman he loves and give her all the comforts and luxuries she deserves."

"I have comfort and luxuries. I want you."

He closed his eyes, unable to face the love shining in hers. How could he explain that he was bound to the customs of his time? That he could no more rely on a woman to support him than he could commit murder? That he had grown accustomed to power and wealth and that he would shrivel and die if he couldn't offer them with all their advantages to the woman he loved? Would she think him shallow and money hungry, or would she understand? He decided not to risk it.

"If our lives are doomed to unhappiness, as Emma suggests," he said, "at least we'll have today to remember."

A smile fluttered at the corners of her mouth, red and swollen from his kisses. "It was memorable, wasn't it?"

A shaft of jealousy stabbed him. "And were the others memorable, too?"

"Others?" Her smile faded.

"Obviously I'm not the first." He hated himself for the truculence in his voice. Who was he to throw stones?

Her smile returned and love for him sparkled in her eyes. "I wasn't a virgin, if that's what you mean."

He struggled against closed-mindedness and lost. "Who was he?"

"No one important." She ran a teasing finger down the bridge of his nose. "I was only eighteen, at college and away from home for the first time in my life. He was a fraternity man, a senior."

"Did you love him?"

"I was young, impressionable—I thought I did. I was dazzled by his good looks and important position on campus. He pursued me until he got what he wanted, another score for the frat house competition, then dropped me. When I understood what had happened, I was happy to be rid of him." Her voice faltered. "Does it matter that much to you?"

As he gazed at her face, he realized nothing mattered but her, that she loved him and that tomorrow he would lose her.

"I was engaged once," he confessed.

"The mysterious Selena?"

He nodded. "Her father and Uncle Cyrus were partners. From childhood we were encouraged to marry. Then, four weeks ago, Selena eloped with a man twice her age—and three times my fortune."

"I'm sorry."

Sunlight danced on her golden hair, kissed the burnished skin of her shoulders and illuminated her eyes. He sat up and gathered her in his arms. "Don't be. She didn't break my heart. She only wounded my pride. I'd never known real love until I met you."

When they broke from their embrace, he reached into his pocket and extracted an ivory-handled penknife. "I want to leave you something for the future, something to remember me by."

He slowly opened the blade and reached toward her. The tempered steel flashed in the sunlight as he buried the knife in the bark beside her head. Then, with painstaking care, he began to carve.

"What is it?" she asked.

"Day after tomorrow is Valentine's Day, and you'll be gone. But if this tree survives the next hundred years, you can find it again when Emma sends you forward in time."

She watched him work, enjoying the firm, steady movements of his hands. When he brushed away the debris and sat back to admire his handiwork, tears rolled down her flushed cheeks.

"Thank you. It's beautiful."

He pulled her into his arms again and stared at the message to the future he'd scored deeply into the oak.

Inside the carved heart he'd engraved, Rand loves Victoria—for all time.

Chapter Eleven

"I'm sick of wearing black." Wrinkling her face in distaste, Tory eyed the jet-beaded evening gown Emma had spread across the bed.

The little woman balled her fists on her hips and glared at Tory with exasperation. "You're supposed to be in mourning for your parents."

"That's—"

"Old-fashioned? Of course it is, but when in Rome..." Emma turned and started rummaging through the bureau drawers. "Where's your corset?"

"I tossed it into the bay." She'd taken great delight in watching the receding tide carry away the instrument of torture.

"You what?" Emma made a clucking sound with her tongue and shook her head. "No matter, there's another here somewhere."

"And if there isn't, I'm sure you'll just poof one out of thin air." Tory lay on her stomach at the foot of the bed and watched Emma scour the room. "How can I consume an eight-course dinner if I'm tied up so tight I can't swallow?''

"Ladies aren't supposed to have appetites," Emma said with a sniff. "Ah, here it is." She extracted a stiff undergarment from the bottom drawer.

Tory rose reluctantly and lifted her arms while Emma tightened the offensive corset around her midriff. She had an appetite, all right. In fact, she was starving. She sighed with pleasure, remembering the long, leisurely afternoon making love with Rand beneath the oaks. What a delicious way to burn calories.

But her happiness dissolved at the thought of her remaining time ticking quickly away. By this time tomorrow, if Angelina and Jason had been united as planned, Rand would be only a memory.

Damn the Victorians and their attitudes toward women. If their society was different, she might stay, knowing the love she and Rand shared stood a chance of lasting a lifetime. If only Emma could help. But although she possessed extraordinary powers, even a fairy godmother couldn't change the entire turn-of-the-century culture to ensure one woman's happiness.

Fidgeting against the confines of the corset, she adjusted the weight of her petticoats. She might learn to accept these ridiculous clothes if she could at least have the satisfaction of her work. Fat chance of that, either.

The women she'd observed at the hotel were little more than mannequins for their stylish clothes, waited on hand and foot by servants, forced to retire to drawing rooms after dinner while the men smoked cigars, drank brandy and discussed business and important events of the day.

Better Rand remember her as she was now than as the unhappy shrew she'd become if she remained. Better she remember him as he'd been that afternoon than grow to resent him as her own personal representative of repressive male society. For someone who called herself a facilitator, Emma had done one heck of a job screwing up their lives.

Yet the pleasant-faced woman standing before her smiled as if she hadn't a clue to the misery she'd caused. Tory sighed. In spite of everything, she couldn't resent the time she'd spent with Rand.

She lifted her arms, then pushed them into the narrow cap sleeves as Emma settled the silk gown over her head. When she turned toward the cheval glass, a stranger peered back at her, an elegant Victorian lady with golden hair arranged in a bouffant crown held in place by exotic wisps of black feathers. The constrictions of the corset molded her figure into an hourglass shape, accentuated by a fitted bodice and a skirt with tucks, pleats and a sweeping train.

When she observed her handiwork, Emma's nose wrinkled. "You're too brown for a woman of your class."

Tory mistrusted the contemplative sparkle of Emma's amethyst eyes.

"Leave my skin alone—"

Too late. A sensation like a thousand tiny needles swept over her body, and when she looked in the mirror again, her complexion gleamed flawlessly white.

"So much for my hard-earned Florida tan," she grumbled.

"Randolph Trent is an extremely wealthy and powerful man," Emma scolded. "Although you're returning to your own time soon, he must maintain his position and reputation in society. Since you are posing as his cousin, anything you do or say will reflect on him long after you're gone. I hope you'll keep that in mind this evening."

Tory nodded as she tugged on black kid gloves that reached above her elbows. Why ladies insisted on covering their arms while baring their shoulders and half their breasts, she'd never understand. She longed to rebel, but Emma spoke the truth. She must do nothing to offend Rand's friends. The last thing she wanted was for him to think badly of her. She tried not to think how her leaving would affect him.

"Move along now." Emma shooed her toward the door. "You mustn't keep the others waiting."

"Aren't you coming?"

She shook her gray curls. "It was kind of Mrs. Fairchild to include me, but I've already sent my regrets. The less I'm seen by humans the better."

"But my chaperon—"

"Mrs. Fairchild and Angelina will fill that responsibility for me."

Tory closed the door behind her with a sigh. Her life was out of control, like a runaway train with Emma at the throttle.

"BY DAMN, that's a handsome woman," a man behind Rand exclaimed.

With a fierce tightening in his chest and a telltale stinging beneath his eyelids, Rand watched Victoria descend the stairs to the lobby. When he'd seen her naked in the sunlight that afternoon, he'd believed she could never look more beautiful, but the sight of her on the staircase robbed him of speech and breath.

Her halo of golden hair, the creamy translucence of her neck and shoulders—unadorned except for a cameo nestled on a black velvet ribbon in the hollow of her throat—and the austere lines of her black gown made the other women in the lobby look like strutting peacocks.

"I say, Trent," Jason Phiswick whispered loudly at his side, "your cousin is a stunner."

"Should I be jealous, Jason?" Angelina asked as she joined them.

Jason whispered his answer in Angelina's ear, and with an approving laugh, she clasped his arm possessively. But Rand's concern was for Victoria.

He met her at the foot of the stairs, lowering his voice so others wouldn't hear. "You look pale. I hope the afternoon wasn't too much for you."

Her aquamarine eyes danced as she shook her head. "Too much? Quite the opposite."

He shot her a devilish grin. "I'll see what I can do to remedy that."

When he offered her his arm, the desire to throw her over his shoulder and carry her upstairs to his suite, dinner party be damned, overcame him. But the sight

of Angelina, laughing and smiling as she stood with
Jason and her parents, reminded him of their mission.
He faced a long evening with Victoria within his reach,
but beyond his grasp.

"Let me introduce you to the others." He resigned
himself to sharing her company.

Tory greeted Angelina, who seemed happier than ever
in the company of Jason, a short, stocky young man
with deep brown eyes, blond hair and a pleasant disposition.

"And this is Mrs. Fairchild," Rand said.

A large woman, dressed in violent purple, reminded
Tory of Barney the Dinosaur in color, size and bovine
features. The stout matron looked down her nose
through a golden lorgnette, her lips puckering with disapproval. "Caswell? I don't believe I know your family."

For Angelina's sake, Tory ignored the woman's
rudeness. "Why should you? My parents lived in Atlanta, and I understand you're from the Midwest."

"Atlanta?" Mrs. Fairchild repeated as if Tory had
said leper colony, then turned away.

Her husband's reaction was more friendly. "Any
relative of Trent's is welcome at our table. Isn't that
right, Angelina?"

The pretty young woman flashed Tory a brilliant
smile. "I'm so glad you could join us." She leaned over,
whispering so the others couldn't hear. "There're not
enough young people here to suit me—most everyone's
my parents' age."

The vivacious girl before her was as different as night from day from the unhappy ghost Tory had previously known. She had to save Angelina from her accident, not only because Emma would then restore Tory to her own time, but because such a girl didn't deserve the misery her premature death had caused.

"Victoria." Rand interrupted her thoughts. "This is Phineas Thibault, another business associate of mine."

A tall, dark-haired man with hawklike features offered her his arm. "May I escort you in to dinner, Miss Caswell?"

As they entered the hotel dining room, Tory caught her breath. The room looked like a set from Martin Scorsese's *The Age of Innocence*. Crystal chandeliers cast a warm glow upward toward ceiling panels of Tiffany stained glass and down on a roomful of elegant people. Men in snowy, starched shirts and dark evening clothes and women whose pale shoulders glowed above rich, jewel-toned fabrics gathered around tables gleaming with fine china, sterling silver and dozens of lighted tapers. Huge epergnes of hothouse blossoms decorated the room, and the delicious aroma of roasted meats and hot breads mingled with the flowers' fragrances.

Tory found herself seated on Fairchild's right at the far end of the table from Rand, who'd been given the place of honor beside Mrs. Fairchild.

Over the first course of green turtle soup, Thibault posed a question to the guests at the table. "Do you think we'll end up at war with the Spanish?"

Memories of high school history classes skittered through Tory's mind. "If the media have their way, you can be sure of it."

"Media?" Jason asked.

The others at the table went silent, turning their attention on Tory.

"The newspapers," she explained. "Yellow journalists are clamoring for war. They'll force us to fight eventually."

Stunned silence reigned at the table. Tory glanced at Rand, wondering what she'd said to provoke such reaction, but found him studying the table as if he'd never seen a soup plate before. A muscle twitched in his cheek.

"Perhaps, Miss Caswell," Mrs. Fairchild announced in an icy voice, "you are unaware that Mr. Thibault owns one of the largest newspapers in Chicago."

Tory turned to the man on her right. "How fascinating. Tell me about your advertising. Who are your biggest clients?"

Thibault choked on his broth. "Why would you be concerned with such matters?"

Tory ignored his patronizing tone. "Advertising has always interested me. Even if someone has the best product in the world, it won't sell if the public doesn't know about it."

At the other end of the table, Mrs. Fairchild raised her voice. "Hasn't the weather been lovely the past few days? Such a relief from February in Chicago."

Fairchild took his cue from his wife. "I saw in the latest Chicago papers where they had three feet of snow."

"Excellent climate here for turkey shooting," Thibault agreed, dismissing Tory. "Why don't we all go hunting next Monday?"

Jason and Fairchild nodded in agreement, and Thibault returned to sipping his soup.

With her cheeks still stinging from his slight, Tory tackled her dinner partner again. "Why won't you answer my question?"

Thibault looked up in surprise. "About advertising? Why would you bother your very pretty head with such matters?"

She disregarded Rand's warning looks. "Who knows, Phineas Thibault? Someday I might wish to open an advertising firm of my own."

"You? A woman?" He laughed raucously, as if he'd been told a risqué joke. "Bad enough you girls think yourselves capable of voting, but running a business? Lord, give me strength!"

Laying a gloved hand on his arm, Tory batted her eyes coquettishly. "Are you a betting man, Phineas?"

At the far end of the table, Rand squirmed and suppressed a smile, obviously enjoying himself.

Thibault dabbed his walrus mustache with his napkin and narrowed his eyes beneath bushy brows. "Why do you ask?"

"Because I'm willing to wager one thousand dollars that women will have the vote within the next twenty-two years." She grinned triumphantly, while Mrs.

Fairchild gasped and Rand, gray eyes twinkling, placed a hand over his mouth, as if to prevent comment.

"Those *women*—one dare not call them ladies," Mrs. Fairchild said with a sneer, "should stay at home where they belong. Their husbands can vote for them."

"What if they don't have husbands, Mama?" Angelina, pretending innocence, threw Tory a sidewise conspiratorial glance.

"*Every* self-respecting lady has a husband," her mother snapped at her.

Angelina's face turned pale, then a deep flush worked its way up her throat and across her cheeks as she glanced toward Jason, who was staring at Thibault.

"What about it, Phineas? Will you take the lady's offer of a wager?" he asked.

"A thousand bucks." Thibault smoothed his mustache with his index finger. "That's quite a sum."

"Larger than I carry with me when I travel," Tory admitted with a wicked grin, "but Cousin Randolph will lend it to me, I'm sure, and Mr. Fairchild can hold the bets."

She flicked a smile down the table, catching Rand's shocked expression.

After a second, the dazed look cleared his face, and he spoke in a hearty tone. "I'll be happy to provide you with the sum, Victoria. And, Phineas, because I trust my cousin's instincts, I'll raise the wager another thousand if you're interested."

You sly devil, Tory thought. *I didn't name you Money Man for nothing.*

Thibault dismissed Tory once more, turned his back to her and leaned down the table toward Rand, extending his hand. "Two thousand dollars it is, Trent. And if the ladies don't have the vote by 1919, you'll owe me the lot."

Satisfied the man would pay dearly for his boorishness, Tory dipped a spoon into her soup.

Across the table, Angelina fidgeted and changed the subject. "Do you have other family, besides your aunt Emma?"

"My sister Jill just married last week. She's moved to Australia with her husband."

"Australia!" Mrs. Fairchild's eyebrows shot up in disapproving peaks. "Did she marry a criminal?"

"Excuse me?" Tory asked.

Mrs. Fairchild's ample bosom heaved as if she addressed a small child. "Isn't Australia where England sends its criminals? I asked if your sister married one?"

Wishing she could smack the pompous woman's fat cheek, Tory counted silently to ten. Judging from Rand's ruddy complexion, his hostess had infuriated him, as well.

Tory struggled to keep an even tone. "Jill married an anthropologist."

"Oh, dear," Mrs. Fairchild said with a condescending sniff.

Tory sighed with frustration. Every word she spoke offended her hostess.

Angelina came to her rescue once more. "Your dress is lovely, Miss Caswell. Do you shop in Atlanta or New York for your clothes?"

"Aunt Emma shops for me. To be honest, I don't know where. She—travels a great deal," Tory replied, thankful for a friendly face.

Rand tried to catch Victoria's eye, but she dropped her gaze to her plate. Splotches of red colored her cheeks, and his heart ached at her discomfort over the slights of Thibault and Mrs. Fairchild. If he'd had any doubts about her unhappiness in his world, the last few minutes had dissolved them. Unintimidated by either position or wealth, she viewed herself as the equal of any man—heresy in his world, and certain to land her in perpetual trouble if she continued as she had that evening. And if she curbed her intelligence and curiosity, she would no longer be his Victoria, the woman he loved.

"Will you be here long, Miss Caswell?" Angelina asked.

"No." The look Victoria sent Rand pierced his soul. "I'm only passing through. I'll be returning home shortly."

"Then I hope to see you again before you go," the young woman said.

"Miss Fairchild," Rand broke in. "I can promise that you will encounter my cousin again before she leaves."

"Wonderful," Angelina said. "You know, it's very strange, Miss Caswell, but I feel as if we've known each other for a long, long time."

Chapter Twelve

Emma's snores rattled through the closed door of her bedroom, thwarting Tory's efforts at sleep. Throwing back the covers, she padded to the doors opening onto the tiny balcony. As she stepped into the night air, the perfume of orange blossoms on the breeze reminded her of the dinner she'd had with Rand on the hotel terrace. Had it only been a few nights before?

Would this be their last night together? Returning to her bed for the blue silk robe draped across its foot, she shrugged the garment over her voluminous white gown and tiptoed to the door.

She paused, listening at the threshold, but Emma's heavy breathing rattled on unabated. Easing open the door, she checked the deserted passageway, then sped on bare feet down the hall to Rand's door.

He opened it almost immediately after her faint knock and pulled her inside, into his arms.

"I hoped you'd come," he murmured against her hair. "Although you really shouldn't—"

"Why should I care about my reputation when I won't be here much longer?"

Strong hands held her at arm's length as he scanned her face in the soft lamplight. "I'm glad you're here. I want to talk to you about reconsidering."

"Reconsidering?"

"About staying here with me," he pleaded. "I'll do anything you want, give you anything you want. I'll fight with you for women's rights, buy you your own advertising company—"

He's right. You'd have everything you could ever wish for—and Rand, too, her heart whispered.

But her head spoke louder. She brushed away his hands and stood at the window, staring out into the darkness. "What good is my own company if no one will do business with me? You saw the attitude of Fairchild and Thibault tonight at dinner. It's men like them who determine a company's success."

His arms circled her waist and he pulled her against him. "What do you care what those men think?"

"I don't care. But I couldn't stay in business without their approval—and that of their wives. And you saw what a hit I made with Mrs. Fairchild." She grimaced at the memory.

His breath warmed the back of her neck. "There has to be some way we could work this out—"

"It's no use." Stifling the voice inside that urged her to give in, to submit to the prejudices of Victorian society, to face anything except leaving him, she struggled against tears. "I came to say goodbye. Let's not quarrel. Who knows how much time we have left?"

She melted against the contours of his hard body thrusting through the fabric of her nightclothes and luxuriated in the heat of his flesh, memorizing every muscle, cataloging every scent of sandalwood, sunshine and the pleasant musky maleness of him, striving to retain every note and cadence of his voice.

He reached across her waist, unknotting the silk sash of her robe and easing it off her shoulders before cupping her breasts through the thin cloth of her gown. Her nipples tightened when his fingers grazed them, and a low moan of pleasure escaped her lips.

"It can't be done." He buried his face in her shoulder, nuzzling her neck.

"What?" Her mind strived to follow his words while her body responded to his touch with tingling awareness in every nerve.

"I can't love you enough in one night to last a lifetime." Turning her toward him, he traced her face with kisses and undid the buttons of her gown, sliding it off until it puddled on the floor around her feet.

"You don't have to," she said breathlessly when he scooped her into his arms. "Come back to my time with me."

After lowering her to the bed, he moved the lamp closer, turning up the flame. "I want to remember you always as you look now."

"Come with me," she repeated.

He ripped his shirt over his head and tossed it aside, then with a swift, deft movement, shoved down his trousers and kicked them away. Stretching out beside her, he leaned over her, his tanned face flushed with passion, his gray eyes smoldering.

"I love you," he whispered, rubbing his jaw against her temple, drawing her body against the length of him, "but, like you, I can't surrender who and what I am."

His lips crushed hers with violent tenderness while his hands explored the curve of her abdomen, the swell of her hip, the sensitive flesh of her thighs. Desire burgeoned within her.

"Please," she urged him.

Rolling onto his back, he positioned her above him, pinioning her, thrusting, pulling her toward him as he suckled her breast, exploring every nook and crevice of her with his fingertips, filling her with his passion. She dug her fingers into his shoulders, moaning in the back of her throat.

Her breathing quickened, matching his gasps. He clutched her to him and cried out, while the lamplight shattered into a thousand stars.

She slumped against his chest, and her perspiration mingled with his as their ragged breaths joined. Cradling her face in his hand, he wiped away her tears with his thumb.

"You're crying?"

"I can't help it."

"Are they sad or happy tears?"

"Both."

With extraordinary tenderness, he smoothed her hair from her face. "No matter what happens in my life from this day forward, this will have been its happiest hour."

He wrapped her in his arms, holding her against him as if he'd never let her go. When his breathing evened, she knew he'd fallen asleep.

Disentangling herself from his arms, she shifted to lie beside him, where she could peruse his sleeping features. With a hesitant finger, she traced the line of his jaw, outlined his lips, swollen from kissing, then drew her fingers down the broad expanse of his chest, across his narrow waist, over the triangle of dark hair toward the hard muscles of his thighs.

Her hair grazed his chest as she brushed his skin with kisses, and when she raised her head, he stared at her with eyes like gray smoke.

"What are you doing?" His husky voice sent her pulses pounding.

"If this is to be the happiest time of your life," she said with a laugh, "we must make it last longer than an hour."

But she wasn't laughing when he rose and covered her body with his own.

Their lovemaking continued throughout the night. Fiercely, tenderly she tried to memorize the feelings, knowing the night must last a lifetime, unwilling to close her eyes for one precious second.

Toward morning, before dawn, a horse clopped down the drive.

"It's the milk wagon," Rand said. "You must return to your room before the other guests awaken."

He sat propped against the headboard, and she lay back in his arms. "I know."

But she didn't move. She couldn't bring herself to leave the warmth of his embrace or the shelter of his bed with its memories of the night's lovemaking.

"Today we must watch over Angelina," he reminded her.

"I know." She clutched him tighter.

"My meeting with Phiswick isn't until this afternoon, but perhaps you'd better ask Angelina to lunch, just to keep an eye on her."

"I will." Her muscles refused to budge. His arms wrapped tighter around her, and his body hardened beneath her.

"When?"

"Later."

"Later?"

"Much later." She turned toward him and lifted her lips to his.

MORNING SUNLIGHT streamed through the windows at the ends of the corridor as Tory scurried to her room. She passed no one in the hall, and when she entered her suite, Emma was gone.

After soaking in a hot bath, she dressed in a crisp white shirtwaist with leg-of-mutton sleeves, a black skirt and sturdy black boots. Grabbing up a straw boater like the one she'd seen Angelina wear in the hotel's historical exhibit, she hurried to the main desk.

"What room is Miss Fairchild in, please?" she asked the desk clerk.

"Suite 242."

"Thanks." She'd started toward the stairs when the clerk called to her.

"If you're looking for Miss Fairchild, she left the hotel a few minutes ago. Said she was going sailing." He lowered his voice discreetly. "Although she didn't look too happy at the prospect."

Panic bubbled in her throat, making speech impossible. She nodded to the clerk, then, hiking her skirt and petticoats to her knees, raced down the hallway to Rand's room and banged on the door.

Rand, his jaw covered in shaving soap, yanked open the door. "What in—"

"No time," she gasped. "Angelina's already left to go sailing."

"Damn and blast!" He jerked her inside, where she stood nervously shifting her weight from one foot to the other while he wiped the later from his face and buttoned his shirt.

"Please hurry," she cried. "If anything happens to her, it will be all my fault."

He shoved his shirt into his trousers, then pulled her toward the door. "Our fault. It took two, didn't it?"

They dashed across the lobby, down the western corridor and onto the portico. At the bottom of the bluff, a sloop bobbed beside the long pier that extended into the bay.

"Angelina!" The strong sea breeze threw Rand's voice back toward them.

They raced to the edge of the bluff and stumbled down the steep stairs to the dock.

"Angelina!" Tory screamed, but wind filled the sail, and the boat heeled over and sped out into the bay.

Their feet pounded against the dock's wooden slats as they dashed to the pier's end, but the sloop had sailed over a hundred yards into the bay.

Tory stood, wringing her hands as she watched the craft depart. An errant gust of wind buffeted the dock, almost knocking her off her feet, and when she looked again, the sloop had capsized.

"My God, she's overboard! She'll drown!" she screamed to Rand.

But he was already jerking off his boots. With a single bound, he jackknifed into the water, swimming toward the struggling girl with long, powerful strokes.

Angelina's tiny form seemed a long way off as Rand plowed through the choppy waters toward her. Her head disappeared beneath the surface twice, and just before Rand reached her, she went under a third time.

Rand dived where she'd last appeared, but when he broke the surface, he was empty-handed.

Tory paced the dock, praying every prayer she knew in between castigating herself for her selfishness. If she hadn't made love with Rand that one last time, she could have caught Angelina before she headed toward the island.

When Rand finally surfaced again, he had Angelina in his grasp. An unmoving, completely still Angelina. Was she dead? Had he found her too late? He tucked her inert form beneath one arm and stroked toward shore with the other. After what seemed an eternity he reached the dock, and Tory leaned down and dragged the unconscious girl onto the rough planks.

The Angelina before her looked like the ghost she'd first met. Her skin paled to chalk white, and blue rimmed her lips. Tory pressed her fingers to the girl's neck but could find no pulse.

Rand levered himself onto the pier and lowered his ear to Angelina's heart. "She's gone."

His eyes, as haunted as those of Angelina's ghost, stared at Tory.

"No!" Tory's scream ripped the heavens, scattering the seabirds from the shore and attracting the guests on the veranda. "She can't die! I won't let her!"

Dropping to her knees, she rolled Angelina onto her stomach and pumped on her back, forcing water from her lungs. While Rand watched, she turned the girl over, tipped back her head and pinched her nostrils. Using every CPR skill her doctor father had taught her, she breathed into the clammy mouth, then pressed with the heel of her hand against Angelina's breastbone.

"She'd dead, I tell you." Rand gripped her shoulder. "Let her go."

Tory shook her head, not breaking her count to speak. Again and again, she breathed into Angelina and compressed her chest. Suddenly the pale lids fluttered. Angelina coughed up water.

"Go for a doctor," Tory told him. "I think she's going to make it."

For a split second, he stared at her, incredulous, then turned on his bare heel and raced up the pier toward the hotel, battling his way through the approaching throng of people.

Angelina's head lolled weakly on Tory's arm, and the girl's pale blue eyes attempted a smile.

"Thank you," she whispered weakly.

Tory smiled. "Everything is going to be all right now."

Jason Phiswick shoved his way through the crowd on the pier and gathered Angelina in his arms. She lay against his shoulder, pale and smiling.

"What happened?" he asked.

"Boating accident. Rand went for the doctor," Tory said, "but I think she's going to be fine."

The fierce look of love he gave Angelina left Tory no doubt that for those two, at least, love would conquer all.

As she watched Jason ascend the steep bluff, carrying Angelina, a hand grabbed her wrist. She turned to find Emma standing beside her.

"No time to waste," the woman said. "Come with me."

"What—"

But Emma jerked her off her feet before she could finish her sentence, and Tory found herself trotting behind Emma up the bluff.

"What's wrong?" Tory asked.

"Nothing's wrong," Emma huffed. "You and Mr. Trent did a splendid job. I can't thank you enough for saving that poor girl from an eternity of torment."

"She'll be okay?"

"She and Jason will live a long and happy life. You can meet their great-grandchildren someday," Emma replied in a breathless voice.

"Where are we going now?"

"No time to explain." Emma yanked her up the veranda steps, into the hotel corridor and through the door of Rand's room.

"It's time," Emma said, adjusting her bonnet and straightening her bodice.

"Time?" Tory's mouth went dry. She knew what Emma meant, but she didn't want to face it. In her frantic efforts to save Angelina, she'd forgotten about her agreement with Emma—that she'd return to her own time if Angelina lived.

"But Rand—"

"He's gone for the doctor. He won't be back for hours." Emma folded her hands at her waist, smiling happily at Tory's distress. Tory would have hit her if she'd thought it would help.

Emma pointed to the wall behind her, and when Tory turned, the solid structure dissolved and her own hotel room appeared behind it.

When the time portal opened, Tory thought of Rand, of never seeing him again. Emma grabbed her arm and tugged her toward the opening.

"Wait," Tory pleaded, "I've changed my mind—"

But Emma's strong hands shoved her through the portal.

"Bon voyage," Emma's cheery voice called as the opening closed behind her.

Tory stumbled and fell, landing in a heap of black bombazine and petticoats on the floor of the closet. She clambered to her feet and beat upon the closet wall until her hands bled, but the structure held firm. Then she slumped to the floor once more, drowning in her own tears.

Chapter Thirteen

Rand crashed into Tory's suite, throwing open the door with such force it banged against the wall.

"Where is she?" he demanded.

Emma, seated at the table in the bay window, put down her teacup and daintily patted her lips with a damask napkin.

"Gone."

The awful finality of the word squeezed the remaining air from his lungs, and he grasped the doorjamb for support. "Gone where?"

She nodded toward the chair across from her. "Come and sit. I'll fix you a drink."

Like a sleepwalker, he stumbled across the room, collapsed into the chair and accepted the drink she poured from a crystal decanter. But his physical exhaustion provided no protection from the pain. He gulped the brandy, choked on the fiery liquid, then slammed his glass onto the tabletop.

Reining in his anger at the woman before him, he asked again, hoping his instincts were wrong. "Where is Victoria?"

"Where she belongs." Emma sipped her tea and studied him over the rim of her china cup. "You both did as I asked, so I fulfilled my promise and returned her to her own time."

He propped his elbows on his knees and supported his heavy head in his hands. After his swim to save Angelina, he'd ridden hell-for-leather into Clearwater Harbor for the doctor, then hurried back as quickly as he could. Now the ache in his heart drove all other sensations from his weary body.

"I didn't have a chance to say goodbye, to tell her I love her one last time."

"Of course not," she said. "I planned it that way. It would have been too distressing, otherwise."

Rage flared through his pain. "This is your fault. If you'd done your job in the first place, Angelina would have been safe, and you wouldn't have dragged us into this mess."

"And you would never have known Victoria Caswell." Emma filled her cup. "Tell me, Mr. Trent. Is it better to have loved and lost than never to have loved at all?"

He glared at her, wishing looks could kill. "Why have you done this to me?"

She reached across the table, picked up a folded newspaper and handed it to him. "Under the circumstances, I think it's time we had a talk about your future."

He raised his arm to shove the paper away, but catching the sight of the date on the masthead, he grabbed it from her hands. "January 25, *1930?* What is this?"

Emma clasped her hands in her lap. "It's your hometown paper. I suggest you read it, particularly the obituaries."

"The obituaries?"

"Death notices."

"I know what they are," he snarled. "But what interest are they to me?"

She nodded toward the paper crumpled in his fist. "You'll find a very familiar name in that paper."

With a vicious snap, he opened the paper and smoothed the page. A bold, black headline jumped out at him: Chicago Financier Dies Penniless.

The blood drained from his face when his own name leapt out from the black-bordered box of print.

"The body of Randolph Cyrus Trent was discovered in a cold-water flat on Chicago's west side. Death, which occurred over a week ago, was from natural causes," he read aloud.

"Tsk, tsk, so sad," she murmured.

Wadding the paper into a ball, he threw it across the table at her. "This was your doing! My life would have turned out fine if you hadn't introduced me to Victoria, then spirited her away. Losing her means losing everything."

Dropping two lumps of sugar into her tea, the little woman shook her head. "You have it all wrong, Mr.

Trent. That newspaper is from your *original* future, before you ever knew Victoria Caswell existed.''

''But it says I died penniless with no family, no friends. How could that happen?''

She poured him another brandy. ''The stock market crashed—will crash in 1929.''

''Crashed?'' He stared at her with glazed eyes. Everything was happening too fast. First Victoria gone, Wall Street doomed to chaos and now his miserable demise forecast.

Emma nodded. ''That crash ushers in the biggest economic depression in this nation's history. You won't be the only one to lose everything. And when you lose your money, your so-called friends will desert you.''

''Phiswick? Fairchild, too?'' He shouldn't have felt so horrified. He'd always considered them as business acquaintances, not friends. Victoria had been the only real friend he'd ever had.

Emma stood and placed her small hand on his bent head. ''I'm sorry, my boy. What the newspaper article doesn't say, thanks to a kindly reporter, is that you took your own life. Turned on the gas jets when you couldn't take the failure or the loneliness anymore.''

His head snapped up. ''Suicide? That's the coward's way out.''

''You had nothing more to live for, I'm afraid,'' she said softly.

''I won't accept that as my future.'' He raked his fingers through his hair and glared at her. ''You said that paper tells my fate *before* I met Victoria. Well, I've met her now, and, by God, if necessary I'll move heaven, earth, and time itself to get her back.''

TORY SHIFTED her weight, banging her elbow on the floor. The pain brought her fully awake. Sunlight streamed through the open blinds of the suite, and she climbed stiffly to her feet. She had fallen asleep on the closet floor, but how long she'd been there, she could only guess. The traitorous Emma had thoroughly scrambled Tory's sense of time.

She rang the front desk. "What day is it?"

"Sunday," the clerk said, "and I have several messages for you, Miss Caswell."

Halfheartedly, she scribbled notes to call Jill and Kristin, then stripped off her clothes and boots and turned on the shower.

Streaming water mixed with her tears and she soaked away the stiffness in her muscles. God knew if the pain in her heart would ever go away. Rand was gone—forever, dead now for years. She could call the Chicago library and ask about his life and death, but did she really want to know if he'd ever married, had a family, or when he died?

When she opened the closet to dress, his clothes hung next to hers. She buried her face in them, inhaling the scent of him that lingered there, piercing her with the memories it evoked. The strength of her love and the depth of her loss had the weight of a century behind them.

She had to get out of the room before she suffocated from grief. After tugging on denim shorts and a University of Georgia sweatshirt, she laced her running shoes. A pain in her stomach reminded her she hadn't eaten in over twenty-four hours, but eating was impossible with the knot of misery blocking her throat.

Sunday morning quiet reigned in the hotel corridor as she sprinted toward the main lobby and out into the sunshine. But the air was different. Layers of haze and pollution hung over the bay—what little of it she could see past the high-rise condominiums. And the pier, where only yesterday she'd breathed life back into Angelina, no longer existed.

Angelina. At least some good had resulted from her misery. Angelina had lived. She wondered if her child had been a boy or a girl? But that child was probably long dead now, too.

Studying the terrain around her, she tried to coordinate her bearings with what they'd been a hundred years before. If she headed south along the bay front, maybe she could pick up the riding trail she and Rand had taken.

She started off, pounding the golf cart track with long strides, hoping if she ran fast enough she could elude the hurt, the emptiness. If nothing else, maybe when she hit a runner's high, she'd ease the pain. Avoiding the early morning golfers, she ran on, not knowing or caring where she headed.

But she couldn't outrun her memories. Rand in her arms, her body joined with his, the one last fleeting look of love he'd given her before he raced away to fetch a doctor for Angelina. When the time portal opened again, she'd told Emma she'd changed her mind. Would she have really stayed if she'd had time to consider? *Yes,* her heart screamed. What good was her life without Rand? Her work couldn't fill that void, couldn't warm her at night, give her children, keep her company in her old age.

When she reached the southern edge of the golf course, she continued onto Bayview Drive, which curved along the waterfront. To her left, luxurious houses enjoyed the water view. On her right, a broad parkway extended from the road to the water.

Money Man, Money Man, Money Man. The phrase pounded in her brain in rhythm with her feet against the asphalt. She'd call Kristin and cancel the Money Man campaign. They'd have to come up with a new idea for Benson, Jurgen and Ives. She hadn't the heart to go forward without Rand.

A sudden cramp in her side made her stop, doubling over to catch her breath. When she lifted her head, the familiarity of her surrounding struck her. The oak grove where she and Rand had made love stretched before her, not nearly as thick and wild as before, but still somehow the same. Hurrying beneath the trees, she realized this place had been her destination all along. The remaining trees were larger, but after a few minutes of study, she located the clearing where they'd shared their picnic and spent the afternoon in each other's arms.

And there on the tree before her was Rand's valentine, blurred by a century of growth, but clearly legible nonetheless—*Rand loves Victoria—for all time.*

She embraced the massive oaken trunk and laid her face against the carving in the rough bark. Her tears returned, shaking her body with their intensity.

"Oh, Rand," she cried, "I would have stayed. If only I'd had a few more minutes to think, I would never have left you."

"Victoria."

The wind sighed her name in his voice and her tears surged stronger. The bark scratched her cheek.

"Victoria," the wind repeated.

A hand touched her shoulder.

She started and turned. Rand stood before her, dressed in a collarless white shirt, jodhpurs and riding boots. Was she dreaming again?

When he lifted her chin and brushed away her tears, the heat of his skin against hers convinced her he was flesh and blood.

"I, too, had second thoughts." He drew her into his arms and kissed her remaining tears away.

She pulled away, searching his face. "What made you change your mind?"

"I missed country music and junk food," he confessed with a laugh.

But when he kissed her again, she had no doubt he missed her most of all.

When she finally came up for breath, she clasped his face in her hands, vowing never again to let him go.

"But how did you get here?" she asked. "And *when* are we?"

Had Emma returned her to 1897? She looked toward the barrier islands where resorts and hotels punctuated the skyline. He'd come to her time.

"You're here in the twentieth century," she said with amazement.

He laughed at the wonder in her feathery voice. "For all time," he promised before kissing her again.

Another musical laugh floated through the oak grove. He raised his head to see Emma, in a tourist's attire of a flowered cotton shift, sandals and a wide-brimmed sun hat, sitting on a bench beneath the oaks, knitting.

"I'm glad you approve, m'dears," she called to them.

"But how?" Tory asked again. "You said you had only one access left to the time portal, and you used that to return me here."

Emma counted stitches on the tiny garment she was knitting, then raised her head and beamed at them.

"What's the fun of being a fairy godmother if one can't bend the rules now and then?"

Epilogue

Tory spread the last of the white frosting on the birthday cake as "Oprah's" theme music floated from the television on the kitchen counter. Wiping her hands on a towel, she focused her attention on the upcoming commercial.

Against a background of Scott Joplin's music, Rand, dressed much as he'd been the morning he first appeared in her bed, sat behind a huge mahogany desk in a Victorian office.

"Making money is what I do." His piercing pewter eyes stared into the camera. "I don't apologize for it."

The scene dissolved to a modern high-rise office with the Atlanta skyline visible through the glass walls behind him. Rand, wearing an Armani suit the color of his eyes, sat on the edge of a chrome and marble desk, repeating his motto.

The camera moved in for a close-up. "If you want to make money, too, consult Benson, Jurgen, Ives and Trent, the investment firm with over a hundred years of experience providing sound advice for its clients."

"Yes!" She pumped her right arm in a victory signal as her eyes teared with pride. In less than two years, Rand had parlayed the remaining money from the sale of his grandfather's watch and coin into a fortune and a partnership with Benson, Jurgen and Ives.

Reviving the Money Man campaign had been his idea—the first big account she'd created since the birth of their daughter, Stephanie. And, trusting her instincts, he'd insisted on performing in the commercials himself.

Steph's laughter rang out in the family room, where she played with her aunt Jill, Uncle Rod and cousin Andy, here from Australia to celebrate her first birthday.

As Tory seated the large pink numeral amidst the pink roses on the cake, the roar of a giant Harley crescendoed down the driveway. From the kitchen window, she watched Rand park his monster machine in the garage.

In the mudroom, he handed her a plastic bag, shucked off his leather jacket and gloves, then pulled her into his arms.

After a few breathless moments, she pulled away, holding up the sack. "You're melting the ice cream."

His grin, even after almost two years of marriage, still made her stomach flip-flop with desire. "That's because you're a hot little number, Mrs. Trent."

She laughed and put the ice cream in the freezer. "Is that any way for a gentleman to talk? The only hot number is the one you'll soon light on your daughter's birthday cake."

Pulling her against him, he nibbled her ear. "I'm not feeling very gentlemanly right now."

Tory turned in his arms and read the desire in his eyes. "Then I'm afraid you'd better take a cold shower, because it's time for Stephanie's party."

The front doorbell chimed in the hall.

"You get your shower," Tory said, "and I'll get the door."

She opened it to find Emma, dressed in a lavender Chanel suit and holding a bag from Neiman-Marcus. "Am I late?"

Tory embraced the little woman and pulled her inside. "The party's just starting."

Emma removed her pillbox hat and patted her gray curls. "I wouldn't miss my favorite goddaughter's first birthday for the world."

Later, Tory gazed out over the garden where the last of the autumn leaves drifted in the twilight, while Stephanie, the feminine image of her handsome father, dozed in her arms, clutching the Victorian doll Emma had given her.

While Rand lit the fire, Jill served coffee to the adults, then pulled an afghan over Andy, asleep on the sofa.

"You've brought life back to this house, Tory," her sister said. "I never thought it would feel like home again after Mom and Dad died."

"Chalk it up to the power of love." Emma stirred sugar into her coffee. "Love can move mountains."

And bend time. Tory met Rand's gaze across the room and smiled contentedly.

"Emma," Jill said, "Tory tells me you're a fortune-teller."

Emma shook her head. "Not really, m'dear. Just a dabbler."

"Give it a try, luv," Rod said. "What's in store for the lot of us?"

Emma's amethyst eyes twinkled. "Well, that's easy enough. Happily ever after—all around."

Rand sat on the arm of Tory's chair, gathering her and his daughter in his arms. When Tory looked up at him, he bent and kissed her forehead, then ruffled Stephanie's curls. His eyes danced, sharing with his wife the secret knowledge of Emma's magic.

"If Emma says happily ever after," he whispered, "we can count on it."

She lifted her face for another kiss. "For all time."

Take 4 bestselling love stories FREE
Plus get a FREE surprise gift!

Special Limited-time Offer

Mail to Harlequin Reader Service®

P.O. Box 609
Fort Erie, Ontario
L2A 5X3

YES! Please send me 4 free Harlequin American Romance® novels and my free surprise gift. Then send me 4 brand-new novels every month, which I will receive months before they appear in bookstores. Bill me at the low price of $3.21 each plus 25¢ delivery and GST*. That's the complete price and a savings of over 10% off the cover prices—quite a bargain! I understand that accepting the books and gift places me under no obligation ever to buy any books. I can always return a shipment and cancel at any time. Even if I never buy another book from Harlequin, the 4 free books and the surprise gift are mine to keep forever.

354 BPA AQTE

Name _____ (PLEASE PRINT)

Address _____ Apt. No. _____

City _____ Province _____ Postal Code _____

STRUMMEL INVESTIGATIONS

American Romance invites you to read Victoria Pade's Strummel Investigations trilogy! Three top-notch P.I.'s in the Strummel family—Quinn, Lindsey and Logan—solve mysteries and find love.

Look for:

#588 THE CASE OF THE BORROWED BRIDE
in June

Quinn Strummel puts his P.I. skills to use when he looks for a missing groom—and accidently falls for the bride!

#590 THE CASE OF THE MAYBE BABIES
in July

Lindsey Strummel helps a bachelor who's found twin infants on his doorstep. Will she solve the mystery—and become a mom?

#594 THE CASE OF THE ACCIDENTAL HEIRESS
in August

Logan Strummel doesn't exactly believe that his new client's had an out-of-body experience—but she's sure got a body *he'd* like to possess!

Strummel Investigations—only from American Romance!